J. G. Ballard

was born in 1930 in Shanghai, China, where his father was a businessman. After the attack on Pearl Harbor, Ballard and his family were placed in a civilian prison camp. They returned to England in 1945. After two years at Cambridge, where he read medicine, Ballard worked as a copywriter and Covent Garden porter before going to Canada with the RAF. In 1956 his first short story was published in *New Worlds* and he took a full-time job on a technical journal, moving on to become assistant editor of a scientific journal, where he stayed until 1961. His first novel, *The Drowned World*, was written in the same year. His acclaimed novel *Empire of the Sun*, first published in 1984, won the *Guardian* Fiction Prize, the James Tait Black Memorial Prize, and was shortlisted for the Booker Prize. It was later filmed by Steven Spielberg. In 1991 J. G. Ballard published the sequel to *Empire of the Sun*, *The Kindness of Women*.

Reviews for *The Venus Hunters* and J. G. Ballard:

'J. G. Ballard writes as though he spent his cradle years sucking a time shifter instead of a teething ring, so proficient is he at creating the four dimensional worlds, concepts and disorientating situations which his characters inhabit. He is at his best here . . . *The Venus Hunters* makes an excellent sampler for those who haven't yet their perceptions teased by Ballard, while those who have enjoyed his full-length works will not be disappointed.'

Short Stories Magazine

'One of the most startling and original novelists' *Time Out*

'A marvellously accomplished stylist with a weirdly creative imagination.' Robert Nye, *Guardian*

'One of the most sensitive and enigmatic novelists of the present day.' *Times Literary Supplement*

Works by J. G. Ballard

THE DROWNED WORLD
THE VOICES OF TIME
THE TERMINAL BEACH
THE DROUGHT
THE CRYSTAL WORLD
THE DAY OF FOREVER
THE VENUS HUNTERS
THE DISASTER AREA
THE ATROCITY EXHIBITION
VERMILION SANDS
CRASH
CONCRETE ISLAND
HIGH-RISE
LOW-FLYING AIRCRAFT
THE UNLIMITED DREAM COMPANY
HELLO AMERICA
MYTHS OF THE NEAR FUTURE
EMPIRE OF THE SUN
RUNNING WILD
THE DAY OF CREATION
WAR FEVER
THE KINDNESS OF WOMEN

J. G. BALLARD

The Venus Hunters

Flamingo
An Imprint of HarperCollins*Publishers*

Flamingo
An Imprint of HarperCollinsPublishers,
77–85 Fulham Palace Road,
Hammersmith, London W6 8JB

Published by Flamingo 1992
9 8 7 6 5 4 3 2 1

First published in Great Britain by Panther Books 1980
Previously published by Granada (Panther)

This collection copyright © J. G. Ballard 1980

Some of the stories in this volume have appeared in a previous Panther
collection under the title of *The Overloaded Man* (1967): 'Now: Zero',
'The Time-Bombs', 'Track 12', 'Passport to Eternity', 'Escapement',
'Time of Passage' and 'The Venus Hunters' copyright © J. G. Ballard 1967;
'The Killing Ground' copyright © J. G. Ballard 1969;
'One Afternoon at Utah Beach' copyright © J. G. Ballard 1978;
'The 60 Minute Zoom' copyright © J. G. Ballard 1976

The Author asserts the moral right to
be identified as the author of this work

ISBN 0 586 05187 2

Set in Plantin

Printed in Great Britain by
HarperCollinsManufacturing Glasgow

Contents

Now: Zero	7
The Time-Tombs	19
Track 12	35
Passport to Eternity	40
Escapement	59
Time of Passage	72
The Venus Hunters	83
The Killing Ground	113
One Afternoon at Utah Beach	121
The 60 Minute Zoom	134

Now: Zero

You ask: how did I discover this insane and fantastic power? Like Dr Faust, was it bestowed upon me by the Devil himself, in exchange for the deed to my soul? Did I, perhaps, acquire it with some strange talismanic object – idol's eyepiece or monkey's paw – unearthed in an ancient chest or bequeathed by a dying mariner? Or, again, did I stumble upon it myself while researching into the obscenities of the Eleusinian Mysteries and the Black Mass, suddenly perceiving its full horror and magnitude through clouds of sulphurous smoke and incense?

None of these. In fact, the power revealed itself to me quite accidentally, during the commonplaces of the everyday round, appearing unobtrusively at my fingertips like a talent for embroidery. Indeed, its appearance was so unheralded, so gradual, that at first I failed to recognize it at all.

But again you ask: why should I tell you this, describe the incredible and hitherto unsuspected sources of my power, freely catalogue the names of my victims, the date and exact manner of their quietus? Am I so mad as to be positively eager for justice – arraignment, the black cap, and the hangman leaping on to my shoulders like Quasimodo, ringing the deathbell from my throat?

No, (consummate irony!) it is the strange nature of my power that I have nothing to fear from broadcasting its secret to all who will listen. I am the power's servant, and in describing it now I still serve it, carrying it faithfully, as you shall see, to its final conclusion.

However, to begin.

Rankin, my immediate superior at the Everlasting Insurance company, became the hapless instrument of the fate which was first to reveal the power to me.

I loathed Rankin. He was bumptious and assertive, innately vulgar, and owed his position solely to an unpleasant cunning and his persistent refusal to recommend me to the directorate for promotion. He had consolidated his position as department manager by marrying a daughter of one of the directors (a dismal harridan, I may add) and was consequently unassailable. Our relationship was based on mutual contempt, but whereas I was prepared to accept my role, confident that my own qualities would ultimately recommend themselves to the directors, Rankin deliberately took advantage of his seniority, seizing every opportunity to offend and denigrate me.

He would systematically undermine my authority over the secretarial staff, who were tacitly under my control, by appointing others at random to the position. He would give me long-term projects of little significance to work on, so segregating me from the rest of the office. Above all, he sought to antagonize me by his personal mannerisms. He would sing, hum, sit uninvited on my desk as he made small talk with the typists, then call me into his office and keep me waiting pointlessly at his shoulder as he read silently through an entire file.

Although I controlled myself, my abomination of Rankin grew remorselessly. I would leave the office seething with anger at his viciousness, sit in the train home with my newspaper opened but my eyes blinded by rage. My evenings and week-ends would be ruined, wastelands of anger and futile bitterness.

Inevitably, thoughts of revenge grew, particularly as I suspected that Rankin was passing unfavourable reports of my work to the directors. Satisfactory revenge, however, was hard to achieve. Finally I decided upon a course I despised, driven to it by desperation: the anonymous letter – not to the directors, for the source would have been too easily discovered, but to Rankin and his wife.

My first letters, the familiar indictments of infidelity, I never posted. They seemed naïve, inadequate, too obviously the handiwork of a paranoiac with a grudge. I locked them away in a small steel box, later re-drafted them, striking out the staler crudities and trying to substitute something more subtle, a hint of perversion and obscenity, that would plunge deeper barbs of suspicion into the reader's mind.

It was while composing the letter to Mrs Rankin, itemizing in an old notebook the more despicable of her husband's qualities, that I discovered the curious relief afforded by the exercise of composition, by the formal statement, in the minatory language of the anonymous letter (which is, certainly, a specialized branch of literature, with its own classical rules and permitted devices) of the viciousness and depravity of the letter's subject and the terrifying nemesis awaiting him. Of course, this catharsis is familiar to those regularly able to recount unpleasant experiences to priest, friend or wife, but to me, who lived a solitary, friendless life, its discovery was especially poignant.

Over the next few days I made a point each evening on my return home of writing out a short indictment of Rankin's iniquities, analysing his motives, and even anticipating the slights and abuses of the next day. These I would cast in the form of narrative, allowing myself a fair degree of licence, introducing imaginary situations and dialogues that served to highlight Rankin's atrocious behaviour and my own stoical forbearance.

The compensation was welcome, for simultaneously Rankin's campaign against me increased. He became openly abusive, criticized my work before junior members of the staff, even threatened to report me to the directors. One afternoon he drove me to such a frenzy that I barely restrained myself from assaulting him. I hurried home, unlocked my writing box and sought relief in my diaries. I wrote page after page, re-enacting in my narrative the day's events, then reaching forward to our final collision the following morning, culminating in an accident that intervened to save me from dismissal.

My last lines were:

. . . Shortly after 2 o'clock the next afternoon, spying from his usual position on the 7th floor stairway for any employees returning late from lunch, Rankin suddenly lost his balance, toppled over the rail and fell to his death in the entrance hall below.

As I wrote this fictitious scene it seemed scant justice, but little did I realize that a weapon of enormous power had been placed gently between my fingers.

Coming back to the office after lunch the next day I was surprised to find a small crowd gathered outside the entrance, a police car and ambulance pulled up by the curb. As I pushed forward up the steps, several policemen emerged from the building clearing the way for two orderlies carrying a stretcher across which a sheet had been drawn, revealing the outlines of a human form. The face was concealed, and I gathered from conversation around me that someone had died. Two of the directors appeared, their faces shocked and drawn.

'Who is it?' I asked one of the office boys who were hanging around breathlessly.

'Mr Rankin,' he whispered. He pointed up the stairwell. 'He slipped over the railing on the 7th floor, fell straight down, completely smashed one of those big tiles outside the lift . . . '

He gabbled on, but I turned away, numbed and shaken by the sheer physical violence that hung in the air. The ambulance drove off, the crowd dispersed, the directors returned, exchanging expressions of grief and astonishment with other members of the staff, the janitors took away their mops and buckets, leaving behind them a damp red patch and the shattered tile.

Within an hour I had recovered. Sitting in front of Rankin's empty office, watching the typists hover helplessly around his desk, apparently unconvinced that their master would never return, my heart began to warm and sing. I became transformed, a load which had threatened to break me had been removed from my back, my mind relaxed, the tensions and bitterness dissipated. Rankin had gone, finally and irrevocably. The era of injustice had ended.

I contributed generously to the memorial fund which made the rounds of the office; I attended the funeral, gloating inwardly as the coffin was bundled into the sod, joining fulsomely in the expressions of regret. I readied myself to occupy Rankin's desk, my rightful inheritance.

My surprise a few days later can easily be imagined when Carter, a younger man of far less experience and generally accepted as my junior, was promoted to fill Rankin's place. At first I was merely baffled, quite unable to grasp the tortuous logic that could so offend all laws of precedence and merit. I assumed that Rankin had done his work of denigrating me only too well.

However, I accepted the rebuff, offered Carter my loyalty and assisted his reorganization of the office.

Superficially these changes were minor. But later I realized that they were far more calculating than at first seemed, and transferred the bulk of power within the office to Carter's hands, leaving me with the routine work, the files of which never left the department or passed to the directors. I saw too that over the previous year Carter had been carefully familiarizing himself with all aspects of my job and was taking credit for work I had done during Rankin's tenure of office.

Finally I challenged Carter openly, but far from being evasive he simply emphasized my subordinate role. From then on he ignored my attempts at a rapprochement and did all he could to antagonize me.

The final insult came when Jacobson joined the office to fill Carter's former place and was officially designated Carter's deputy.

That evening I brought down the steel box in which I kept record of Rankin's persecutions and began to describe all that I was beginning to suffer at the hands of Carter.

During a pause the last entry in the Rankin diary caught my eye:

. . . Rankin suddenly lost his balance, toppled over the rail and fell to his death in the entrance hall below.

The words seemed to be alive, they had strangely vibrant overtones. Not only were they a remarkably accurate forecast of Rankin's fate, but they had a distinctly magnetic and compulsive power that separated them sharply from the rest of the entries. Somewhere within my mind a voice, vast and sombre, slowly intoned them.

On a sudden impulse I turned the page, found a clean sheet and wrote:

The next afternoon Carter died in a street accident outside the office.

What childish game was I playing? I was forced to smile at myself, as primitive and irrational as a Haitian witch doctor transfixing a clay image of his enemy.

I was sitting in the office the following day when the squeal of tyres in the street below riveted me to my chair. Traffic stopped abruptly and there was a sudden hubbub followed by silence. Only Carter's office overlooked the street; he had gone out half an hour earlier so we pressed past his desk and leaned out through the window.

A car had skidded sharply across the pavement and a group of ten or a dozen men were lifting it carefully back on to the roadway. It was undamaged but what appeared to be oil was leaking sluggishly into the gutter. Then we saw the body of a man outstretched beneath the car, his arms and head twisted awkwardly.

The colour of his suit was oddly familiar.

Two minutes later we knew it was Carter.

That night I destroyed my notebook and all records I had made about Rankin's behaviour. Was it coincidence, or in some way had I willed his death, and in the same way Carter's? Impossible – no conceivable connection could exist between the diaries and the two deaths, the pencil marks on the sheets of paper were arbitrary curved lines of graphite, representing ideas which existed only in my mind.

But the solution to my doubts and speculations was too obvious to be avoided.

I locked the door, turned a fresh page of the notebook and cast round for a suitable subject. I picked up my evening paper. A young man had just been reprieved from the death penalty for the murder of an old woman. His face stared from a photograph coarse, glowering, conscienceless.

I wrote:

Frank Taylor died the next day in Pentonville Prison.

The scandal created by Taylor's death almost brought about the resignations of both the Home Secretary and the Prison Commissioners. During the next few days violent charges were levelled in all directions by the newspapers, and it finally transpired that Taylor had been brutally beaten to death by his warders. I carefully read the evidence and findings of the tribunal of enquiry when they were published, hoping that they might throw some light on the extraordinary and malevolent agency which linked the statements in my diaries with the inevitable deaths on the subsequent day.

However, as I feared, they suggested nothing. Meanwhile I sat quietly in my office, automatically carrying out my work, obeying Jacobson's instructions without comment, my mind elsewhere, trying to grasp the identity and import of the power bestowed on me.

Still unconvinced, I decided on a final test, in which I would give precisely detailed instructions, to rule out once and for all any possibility of coincidence.

Conveniently, Jacobson offered himself as my subject.

So, the door locked securely behind me, I wrote with trembling fingers, fearful lest the pencil wrench itself from me and plunge into my heart.

Jacobson died at 2.43 P.M. the next day after slashing his wrists with a razor blade in the second cubicle from the left in the men's washroom on the third floor.

I sealed the notebook into an envelope, locked it into the box and lay awake through a sleepless night, the words echoing in my ears, glowing before my eyes like jewels of Hell.

After Jacobson's death – exactly according to my instructions – the staff of the department were given a week's holiday (in part to keep them away from curious newspapermen, who were beginning to scent a story, and also because the directors believed that Jacobson had been morbidly influenced by the deaths of Rankin and Carter). During those seven days I chafed impatiently to return to work. My whole attitude to the power had undergone a considerable change. Having to my own satisfaction verified its existence, if not its source, my mind turned again towards the future. Gaining confidence, I realized that if I had been bequeathed the power it was my obligation to restrain any fears and make use of it. I reminded myself that I might be merely the tool of some greater force.

Alternatively, was the diary no more than a mirror which revealed the future, was I in some fantastic way twenty-four hours ahead of time when I described the deaths, simply a recorder of events that had already taken place?

These questions exercised my mind ceaselessly.

On my return to work I found that many members of the staff had resigned, their places being filled only with difficulty, news of the three deaths, particularly Jacobson's suicide, having reached the newspapers. The directors' appreciation of those senior members of the staff who remained with the firm I was able to turn to good account in consolidating my position. At last I took over command of the department – but this was no more than my due, and my eyes were now set upon a directorship.

All too literally, I would step into dead men's shoes.

Briefly, my strategy was to precipitate a crisis in the affairs of the firm which would force the board to appoint new executive directors from the ranks of the department managers. I therefore waited until a week before the next meeting of the board, and then wrote out four slips of paper, one for each of the executive directors. Once a director I should be in a position to propel myself rapidly to the chairmanship of the board, by appointing my own candidates to vacancies as they successively appeared. As chairman I should automatically find a seat on the board of the parent company, there to repeat the process, with whatever variations necessary. As soon as real power came within my orbit my rise to absolute national, and ultimately global, supremacy would be swift and irreversible.

If this seems naïvely ambitious, remember that I had as yet failed to appreciate the real dimensions and purpose of the power, and still thought in the categories of my own narrow world and background.

A week later, as the sentences on the four directors simultaneously expired, I sat calmly in my office, reflecting upon the brevity of human life, waiting for the inevitable summons to the board. Understandably, the news of their deaths, in a succession of motorcar accidents, brought general consternation upon the office, of which I was able to take advantage by retaining the only cool head.

To my amazement the next day I, with the rest of the staff, received a month's pay in lieu of notice. Completely flabbergasted – at first I feared that I had been discovered – I protested volubly to the chairman, but was assured that although everything I had done was deeply appreciated, the firm was nonetheless no longer able to support itself as a viable unit and was going into enforced liquidation.

A farce indeed! So a grotesque justice had been done. As I left the office for the last time that morning I realized that in future I must use my power ruthlessly. Hesitation, the exercise of scruple, the calculation of niceties – these merely made me all the more vulnerable to the inconstancies and barbarities of fate. Henceforth I would be brutal, merciless, bold. Also, I must not delay. The power might wane, leave me defenceless, even less fortunately placed than before it revealed itself.

My first task was to establish the power's limits. During the next week I carried out a series of experiments to assess its capacity, working my way progressively up the scale of assassination.

It happened that my lodgings were positioned some two or three hundred feet below one of the principal airlanes into the city. For years I had suffered the nerve-shattering roar of airliners flying in overhead at two-minute intervals, shaking the walls and ceiling, destroying thought. I took down my notebooks. Here was a convenient opportunity to couple research with redress.

You wonder did I feel no qualms of conscience for the 75 victims who hurtled to their deaths across the evening sky twenty-four hours later, no sympathy for their relatives, no doubts as to the wisdom of wielding my power indiscriminately?

I answer: No! Far from being indiscriminate I was carrying out an experiment vital to the furtherance of my power.

I decided on a bolder course. I had been born in Stretchford, a mean industrial slum that had done its best to cripple my spirit and body. At last it could justify itself by testing the efficacy of the power over a wide area.

In my notebook I wrote the short flat statement:

Every inhabitant of Stretchford died at noon the next day.

Early the following morning I went out and bought a radio, sat by it patiently all day, waiting for the inevitable interruption of the afternoon programmes by the first horrified reports of the vast Midland holocaust.

Nothing, however, was reported! I was astonished, the orientations of my mind disrupted, its very sanity threatened. Had my power dissipated itself, vanishing as quickly and unexpectedly as it had appeared?

Or were the authorities deliberately suppressing all mention of the cataclysm, fearful of national hysteria?

I immediately took the train to Stretchford.

At the station I tactfully made inquiries, was assured that the city was firmly in existence. Were my informants, though, part of the government's conspiracy of silence, was it aware that a monstrous agency was at work, and was somehow hoping to trap it?

But the city was inviolate, its streets filled with traffic, the smoke of countless factories drifting across the blackened rooftops.

I returned late that evening, only to find my landlady importuning me for my rent. I managed to postpone her demands for a day, promptly unlocked my diary and passed sentence upon her, praying that the power had not entirely deserted me.

The sweet relief I experienced the next morning when she was discovered at the foot of the basement staircase, claimed by a sudden stroke, can well be imagined.

So my power still existed!

★ ★ ★

15

During the succeeding weeks its principal features disclosed themselves. First, I discovered that it operated only within the bounds of feasibility. Theoretically the simultaneous deaths of the entire population of Stretchford might have been effected by the coincident explosions of several hydrogen bombs, but as this event was itself apparently impossible (hollow, indeed, are the boastings of our militarist leaders) the command was never carried out.

Secondly, the power entirely confined itself to the passage of the sentence of death. I attempted to control or forecast the motions of the stock market, the results of horse races, the behaviour of my employers at my new job – all to no avail.

As for the sources of the power, these never revealed themselves. I could only conclude that I was merely the agent, the willing clerk, of some macabre nemesis struck like an arc between the point of my pencil and the vellum of my diaries

Sometimes it seemed to me that the brief entries I made were cross-sections through the narrative of some vast book of the dead existing in another dimension, and that as I made them my handwriting overlapped that of a greater scribe's along the narrow pencilled line where our respective planes of time crossed each other, instantly drawing from the eternal banks of death a final statement of account on to some victim within the tangible world around me.

The diaries I kept securely sealed within a large steel safe and all entries were made with the utmost care and secrecy, to prevent any suspicion linking me with the mounting catalogue of deaths and disasters. The majority of these were effected solely for purposes of experiment and brought me little or no personal gain.

It was therefore all the more surprising when I discovered that the police had begun to keep me under sporadic observation.

I first noticed this when I saw my landlady's successor in surreptitious conversation with the local constable, pointing up the stairs to my room and making head-tapping motions, presumably to indicate my telepathic and mesmeric talents. Later, a man whom I can now identify as a plainclothes detective stopped me in the street on some flimsy pretext and started a wandering conversation about the weather, obviously designed to elicit information.

No charges were ever laid against me, but subsequently my employers also began to watch me in a curious manner. I therefore assumed that the possession of the power had invested me with a distinct and visible aura, and it was this that stimulated curiosity.

As this aura became detectable by greater and greater numbers of people – it would be noticed in bus queues and cafes – and the first oblique, and for some puzzling reason, amused references to it were made openly by members of the public, I knew that the power's period of utility was ending. No longer would I be able to exercise it without fear of detection. I should have to destroy the diary, sell the safe which so long had held its secret, probably even refrain from ever thinking about the power lest this alone generate the aura.

To be forced to lose the power, when I was only on the threshold of its potential, seemed a cruel turn of fate. For reasons which still remained closed to me, I had managed to penetrate behind the veil of commonplaces and familiarity which masks the inner world of the timeless and the preternatural. Must the power, and the vision it revealed, be lost forever?

This question ran through my mind as I looked for the last time through my diary. It was almost full now, and I reflected that it formed one of the most extraordinary texts, if unpublished, in the history of literature. Here, indeed, was established the primacy of the pen over the sword!

Savouring this thought, I suddenly had an inspiration of remarkable force and brilliance. I had stumbled upon an ingenious but simple method of preserving the power in its most impersonal and lethal form without having to wield it myself and itemize my victims' names.

This was my scheme: I would write and have published an apparently fictional story in conventional narrative in which I would describe, with complete frankness, my discovery of the power and its subsequent history. I would detail precisely the names of my victims, the mode of their deaths, the growth of my diary and the succession of experiments I carried out. I would be scrupulously honest, holding nothing back whatsoever. In conclusion I would tell of my decision to abandon the power and publish a full and dispassionate account of all that had happened.

Accordingly, after a considerable labour, the story was written and published in a magazine of wide circulation.

You show surprise? I agree; as such I should merely have been

17

signing my own death warrant in indelible ink and delivering myself straight to the gallows. However, I omitted a single feature of the story: its denouement, or surprise ending, the twist in its tail. Like all respectable stories, this one too had its twist, indeed one so violent as to throw the earth itself out of its orbit. This was precisely what it was designed to do.

For the twist in this story was that it contained my last command to the power, my final sentence of death.

Upon whom? Who else, but upon the story's reader!

Ingenious, certainly, you willingly admit. As long as issues of the magazine remain in circulation (and their proximity to victims of this extraordinary plague guarantees that) the power will continue its task of annihilation. Its author alone will remain unmolested, for no court will hear evidence at second hand, and who will live to give it at first hand?

But where, you ask, was the story published, fearful that you may inadvertently buy the magazine and read it.

I answer: Here! It is the story that lies before you now. Savour it well, its finish is your own. As you read these last few lines you will be overwhelmed by horror and revulsion, then by fear and panic. Your heart seizes, its pulse falling . . . your mind clouds . . . your life ebbs . . . you are sinking, within a few seconds you will join eternity . . . three . . . two . . . one . . .

Now!

Zero.

The Time-Tombs

I

Usually in the evenings, while Traxel and Bridges drove off into the sand-sea, Shepley and the Old Man would wander among the gutted time-tombs, listening to them splutter faintly in the dying light as they recreated their fading personas, the deep crystal vaults flaring briefly like giant goblets.

Most of the time-tombs on the southern edge of the sand-sea had been stripped centuries earlier. But Shepley liked to saunter through the straggle of half-submerged pavilions, the warm ancient sand playing over his bare feet like wavelets on some endless beach. Alone among the flickering tombs, with the empty husks of the past ten thousand years, he could temporarily forget his nagging sense of failure.

Tonight, however, he would have to forego the walk. Traxel, who was nominally the leader of the group of tomb-robbers, had pointedly warned him at dinner that he must pay his way or leave. For three weeks Shepley had put off going with Traxel and Bridges, making a series of progressively lamer excuses, and they had begun to get impatient with him. The Old Man they would tolerate, for his vast knowledge of the sand-sea – he had combed the decaying tombs for over forty years and knew every reef and therm-pool like the palm of his hand – and because he was an institution that somehow dignified the lowly calling of tomb-robber, but Shepley had been there for only three months and had nothing to offer except his morose silences and self-hate.

'Tonight, Shepley,' Traxel told him firmly in his hard clipped voice, 'you must find a tape. We cannot support you indefinitely. Remember, we're all as eager to leave Vergil as you are.'

Shepley nodded, watching his reflection in the gold finger-bowl. Traxel sat at the head of the tilting table, his high-collared velvet jacket unbuttoned. Surrounded by the battered gold plate filched from the tombs, red wine spilling across the table from Bridges' tankard, he looked more like a Renaissance princeling than a cashiered PhD. Once Traxel had been a Professor of Semantics, and Shepley wondered what scandal had brought him to Vergil. Now, like a grave-rat, he hunted the time-tombs with Bridges, selling the tapes to the Psycho-History Museums at a dollar a foot. Shepley found it impossible to come to terms with the tall, aloof man. By contrast Bridges, who was just a thug, had a streak of blunt good humour that made him tolerable, but with Traxel he could never relax. Perhaps his cold, laconic manner represented authority, the high-faced, stern-eyed interrogators who still pursued Shepley in his dreams.

Bridges kicked back his chair and lurched away around the table, pounding Shepley across the shoulders.

'You come with us, kid. Tonight we'll find a megatape.'

Outside, the low-hulled, camouflaged halftrack waited in a saddle between two dunes. The old summer palace was sinking slowly below the desert, and the floor of the banqueting hall shelved into the white sand like the deck of a subsiding liner, going down with lights blazing from its staterooms.

'What about you, Doctor?' Traxel asked the Old Man as Bridges swung aboard the half-track and the exhaust kicked out. 'It would be a pleasure to have you along.' When the Old Man shook his head Traxel turned to Shepley. 'Well, are you coming?'

'Not tonight,' Shepley demurred hurriedly. 'I'll, er, walk down to the tomb-beds later myself.'

'Twenty miles?' Traxel reminded him, watching reflectively. 'Very well.' He zipped up his jacket and strode away towards the half-track. As they moved off he shouted 'Shepley, I meant what I said!'

Shepley watched them disappear among the dunes. Flatly, he repeated 'He means what he says.'

The Old Man shrugged, sweeping some sand off the table. 'Traxel . . . he's a difficult man. What are you going to do?' The note of reproach in his voice was mild, realizing that Shepley's motives were the same as those which had marooned himself on the lost beaches of the sand-sea four decades earlier.

Shepley snapped irritably. 'I can't go with him. After five minutes he drains me like a skull. What's the matter with Traxel? Why is he here?'

The Old Man stood up, staring out vaguely into the desert. 'I can't remember. Everyone has his own reasons. After a while the stories overlap.'

They walked out under the proscenium, following the grooves left by the half-track. A mile away, winding between the last of the lavalakes which marked the southern shore of the sand-sea, they could just see the vehicle vanishing into the darkness. The old tomb-beds, where Shepley and the Old Man usually walked, lay between them, the pavilions arranged in three lines along a low basaltic ridge. Occasionally a brief flare of light flickered up into the white, bone-like darkness, but most of the tombs were silent.

Shepley stopped, hands falling limply to his sides. 'The new beds are by the Lake of Newton, nearly twenty miles away. I can't follow them.'

'I shouldn't try,' the Old Man rejoined. 'There was a big sand-storm last night. The time-wardens will be out in force marking any new tombs uncovered.' He chuckled softly to himself. 'Traxel and Bridges won't find a foot of tape – they'll be lucky if they're not arrested.' He took off his white cotton hat and squinted shrewdly through the dead light, assessing the altered contours of the dunes, then guided Shepley towards the old mono-rail whose southern terminus ended by the tomb-beds. Once it had been used to transport the pavilions from the station on the northern shore of the sand-sea, and a small gyro-car still leaned against the freight platform. 'We'll go over to Pascal. Something may have come up, you never know.'

Shepley shook his head. 'Traxel took me there when I first arrived. They've all been stripped a hundred times.'

'Well, we'll have a look.' The Old Man plodded on towards the mono-rail, his dirty white suit flapping in the low breeze. Behind them the summer palace – built three centuries earlier by a business tycoon from Ceres – faded into the darkness, the rippling glass tiles in the upper spires merging into the starlight.

Propping the car against the platform, Shepley wound up the gyroscope, then helped the Old Man on to the front seat. He pried off a piece of rusting platform rail and began to punt the car away. Every fifty yards or so they stopped to clear the sand that submerged the track, but slowly they wound off among the dunes and lakes, here and there the onion-shaped cupola of a solitary time-tomb rearing up into the sky beside them, fragments of the crystal casements twinkling in the sand like minuscule stars.

Half an hour later, as they rode down the final long incline towards the Lake of Pascal, Shepley went forward to sit beside the Old Man, who emerged from his private reverie to ask quizzically. 'And you, Shepley, why are you here?'

Shepley leaned back, letting the cool air drain the sweat off his face. 'Once I tried to kill someone,' he explained tersely. 'After they cured me I found I wanted to kill myself instead.' He reached down to the hand-brake as they gathered speed. 'For ten thousand dollars I can go back on probation. Here I thought there would be a freemasonry of sorts. But then you've been kind enough, Doctor.'

'Don't worry, we'll get you a winning tape.' He leaned forward, shielding his eyes from the stellar glare, gazing down at the little cantonment of gutted time-tombs on the shore of the lake. In all there were about a dozen pavilions, their roofs holed, the group Traxel had shown to Shepley after his arrival when he demonstrated how the vaults were robbed.

'Shepley! Look, lad!'

'Where? I've seen them before, Doctor. They're stripped.'

The Old Man pushed him away. 'No, you fool, about three hundred yards to the west, in the shadow of the long ridge where the big dunes have moved. Can you see them now?' He drummed a white fist on Shepley's knee. 'You've made it, lad. You won't need to be frightened of Traxel or anyone else now.'

Shepley jerked the car to a halt. As he ran ahead of the Old Man towards the escarpment he could see several of the time-tombs glowing along the sky lines, emerging briefly from the dark earth like the tents of some spectral caravan.

II

For ten millenia the Sea of Vergil had served as a burial ground, and the 1,500 square miles of restless sand were estimated to contain over twenty thousand tombs. All but a minute fraction had been stripped by the successive generations of tomb robbers, and an intact spool of the 17th Dynasty could now be sold to the Psycho-History Museum at Tycho for over 3,000 dollars. For each preceding dynasty, though none older than the 12th had ever been found, there was a bonus.

There were no corpses in the time-tombs, no dusty skeletons. The cyber-architectonic ghosts which haunted them were embalmed in the metallic codes of memory tapes, three-dimensional molecular transcriptions of their living originals, stored among the dunes as a stupendous act of faith, in the hope that one day the physical re-creation of the coded personalities would be possible. After five thousand years the attempt had been reluctantly abandoned, but out of respect for the tomb-builders their pavilions were left to take their own hazard with time in the Sea of Vergil. Later the tomb-robbers had arrived, as the historians of the new epochs realized the enormous archives that lay waiting for them in this antique limbo. Despite the time-wardens, the pillaging of the tombs and the illicit traffic in dead souls continued.

'Doctor! Come on! Look at them!'

Shepley plunged wildly up to his knees in the silver-white sand, diving from one pavilion to the next like a frantic puppy.

Smiling to himself, the Old Man climbed slowly up the melting slope, submerged to his waist as the fine crystals poured away around him, feeling for spurs of firmer rock. The cupola of the nearest tomb tilted into the sky, only the top six inches of the casements visible below the overhang. He sat for a moment on the roof, watching Shepley dive about in the darkness, then peered through the casement, brushing away the sand with his hands.

The tomb was intact. Inside he could see the votive light burning over the altar, the hexagonal nave with its inlaid gold floor and drapery, the narrow chancel at the rear which held the memory store. Low tables surrounded the chancel, carrying beaten goblets and gold bowls, token offerings intended to distract any pillager who stumbled upon the tomb.

Shepley came leaping over to him. 'Let's get into them, Doctor! What are we waiting for?'

The Old Man looked out over the plain below, at the cluster of stripped tombs by the edge of the lake, at the dark ribbon of the gyro-rail winding away among the hills. The thought of the fortune that lay at his fingertips left him unmoved. For so long now he had lived among the tombs that he had begun to assume something of their ambience of immortality and timelessness, and Shepley's impatience seemed to come out of another dimension. He hated stripping the tombs. Each one robbed represented, not just the final extinction of a surviving personality, but a diminution of his own sense of eternity. Whenever a new tomb-bed emerged from the sand he felt something within himself momentarily rekindled, not hope, for he was beyond that, but a serene acceptance of the brief span of time left to him.

'Right,' he nodded. They began to cleave away the sand piled around the door, Shepley driving it down the slope where it spilled in a white foam over the darker basaltic chips. When the narrow portico was free the Old Man squatted by the timeseal. His fingers cleaned away the crystals embedded between the tabs, then played lightly over them.

Like dry sticks breaking, an ancient voice crackled

> Orion, Betelgeuse, Altair,
> What twice-born star shall be my heir,
> Doomed again to be this scion –

'Come on, Doctor, this is a quicker way.' Shepley put one leg up against the door and lunged against it futilely. The Old Man pushed him away. With his mouth close to the seal, he rejoined.

> 'Of Altair, Betelgeuse, Orion.'

As the doors accepted this and swung back he murmured:

'Don't despise the old rituals. Now, let's see.' They paused in the cool, unbreathed air, the votive light throwing a pale ruby glow over the gold drapes parting across the chancel.

The air became curiously hazy and mottled. Within a few seconds it began to vibrate with increasing rapidity, and a succession of vivid colours rippled across the surface of what appeared to be a cone of light projected from the rear of the chancel. Soon this resolved itself into a three-dimensional image of an elderly man in a blue robe.

Although the image was transparent, the brilliant electric blue of the robe revealing the inadequacies of the projection system, the intensity of the illusion was such that Shepley almost expected the man to speak to them. He was well into his seventies, with a composed, watchful face and thin grey hair, his hands resting quietly in front of him. The edge of the desk was just visible, the proximal arc of the cone enclosing part of a silver ink-stand and a small metal trophy. These details, and the spectral bookshelves and paintings which formed the backdrop of the illusion, were of infinite value to the Psycho-History institutes, providing evidence of the earlier

24

civilizations far more reliable than the funerary urns and goblets in the anteroom.

Shepley began to move forward, the definition of the persona fading slightly. A visual relay of the memory store, it would continue to play after the code had been removed, though the induction coils would soon exhaust themselves. Then the tomb would be finally extinct.

Two feet away, the wise unblinking eyes of the long dead magnate stared at him steadily, his seamed forehead like a piece of pink transparent wax. Tentatively, Shepley reached out and plunged his hand into the cone, the myriad vibration patterns racing across his wrist. For a moment he held the dead man's face in his hand, the edge of the desk and the silver inkstand dappling across his sleeve.

Then he stepped forward and walked straight through him into the darkness at the rear of the chancel.

Quickly, following Traxel's instructions, he unbolted the console containing the memory store, lifting out the three heavy drums which held the tape spools. Immediately the persona began to dim, the edge of the desk and the bookshelves vanishing as the cone contracted. Narrow bands of dead air appeared across it, one, at the level of the man's neck, decapitating him. Lower down the scanner had begun to misfire. The folded hands trembled nervously, and now and then one of his shoulders gave a slight twitch. Shepley stepped through him without looking back.

The Old Man was waiting outside. Shepley dropped the drums on to the sand. 'They're heavy,' he muttered. Brightening, he added 'There must be over five hundred feet here, Doctor. With the bonus, and all the others as well – ' He took the Old Man's arm. 'Come on, let's get into the next one.'

The Old Man disengaged himself, watching the sputtering persona in the pavilion, the blue light from the dead man's suit pulsing across the sand like a soundless lightning storm.

'Wait a minute, lad, don't run away with yourself.' As Shepley began to slide off through the sand, sending further falls down the slope, he added in a firmer voice 'And stop moving all that sand around! These tombs have been hidden here for ten thousand years. Don't undo all the good work, or the wardens will be finding them the first time they go past.'

'Or Traxel,' Shepley said, sobering quickly. He glanced around the lake below, searching the shadows among the tombs in case anyone was watching them, waiting to seize the treasure.

III

The Old Man left him at the door of the next pavilion, reluctant to watch the tomb being stripped of the last vestige of its already meagre claim to immortality.

'This will be our last one tonight,' he told Shepley. 'You'll never hide all these tapes from Bridges and Traxel.'

The furnishings of the tomb differed from that of the previous one. Sombre black marble panels covered the walls, inscribed with strange gold-leaf hieroglyphs, and the inlays in the floor represented stylized astrological symbols, at once eerie and obscure. Shepley leaned against the altar, watching the cone of light reach out towards him from the chancel as the curtains parted. The predominant colours were gold and carmine, mingled with a vivid powdery copper that gradually resolved itself into the huge, harp-like head-dress of a reclining woman. She lay in the centre of what seemed to be a sphere of softly luminous gas, inclined against a massive black catafalque, from the sides of which flared two enormous heraldic wings. The woman's copper hair was swept straight back from her forehead, some five or six feet long, and merged with the plumage of the wings, giving her an impression of tremendous contained speed, like a goddess arrested in a moment of flight in a cornice of some great temple-city of the dead.

Her eyes stared forward expressionlessly at Shepley. Her arms and shoulders were bare, and the white skin, like compacted snow, had a brilliant surface sheen, the reflected light glaring against the black base of the catafalque and the long sheath-like gown that swept around her hips to the floor. Her face, like an exquisite porcelain mask, was tilted upward slightly, the half-closed eyes suggesting that the woman was asleep or dreaming. No background had been provided for the image, but the bowl of luminescence invested the persona with immense power and mystery.

Shepley heard the Old Man shuffle up behind him.

'Who is she, Doctor? A princess?'

The Old Man shook his head slowly. 'You can only guess. I don't know. There are strange treasures in these tombs. Get on with it, we'd best be going.'

Shepley hesitated. He started to walk towards the woman on the catafalque, and then felt the enormous upward surge of her flight, the pressure of all the past centuries carried before her brought to a sudden focus in front of him, holding him back like a physical barrier.

'Doctor!' He reached the door just behind the Old Man. 'We'll leave this one, there's no hurry!'

The Old Man examined his face shrewdly in the moonlight, the brilliant colours of the persona flickering across Shepley's youthful cheeks. 'I know how you feel, lad, but remember, the woman doesn't exist, any more than a painting. You'll have to come back for her soon.'

Shepley nodded quickly. 'I know, but some other night. There's something uncanny about this tomb.' He closed the doors behind them, and immediately the huge cone of light shrank back into the chancel, sucking the woman and the catafalque into the darkness. The wind swept across the dunes, throwing a fine spray of sand on to the half-buried cupolas, sighing among the wrecked tombs.

The Old Man made his way down to the mono-rail, and waited for Shepley as he worked for the next hour, slowly covering each of the tombs.

On the Old Man's recommendation he gave Traxel only one of the canisters, containing about 500 feet of tape. As prophesied, the time-wardens had been out in force in the Sea of Newton, and two members of another gang had been caught red-handed. Bridges was in foul temper, but Traxel, as ever self-contained, seemed unworried at the wasted evening.

Straddling the desk in the tilting ballroom, he examined the drum with interest, complimenting Shepley on his initiative. 'Excellent, Shepley. I'm glad you joined us now. Do you mind telling me where you found this?'

Shepley shrugged vaguely, began to mumble something about a secret basement in one of the gutted tombs nearby, but the Old Man cut in: 'Don't broadcast it everywhere! Traxel, you shouldn't ask questions like that – he's got his own living to earn.'

Traxel smiled, sphinx-like. 'Right again, Doctor.' He tapped the smooth untarnished case. 'In mint condition, and a 15th Dynasty too.'

'Tenth!' Shepley claimed indignantly, frightened that Traxel might try to pocket the bonus. The Old Man cursed, and Traxel's eyes gleamed.

'Tenth, is it? I didn't realize there were any 10th Dynasty tombs still intact. You surprise me, Shepley. Obviously you have concealed talents.'

Luckily he seemed to assume that the Old Man had been hoarding the tape for years.

Face down in a shallow hollow at the edge of the ridge, Shepley watched the white-hulled sand-car of the time-wardens shunt through the darkness by the old cantonment. Directly below him jutted the spires of the newly discovered tomb-bed, invisible against the dark background of the ridge. The two wardens in the sand-car were more interested in the old tombs; they had spotted the gyro-car lying on its side by the mono-rail, and guessed that the gangs had been working the ruins over again. One of them stood on the running board, flicking a torch into the gutted pavilions. Crossing the mono-rail, the car moved off slowly across the lake to the northwest, a low pall of dust settling behind it.

For a few moments Shepley lay quietly in the slack darkness, watching the gullies and ravines that led into the lake, then slid down among the pavilions. Brushing away the sand to reveal a square wooden plank, he slipped below it into the portico.

As the golden image of the enchantress loomed out of the black-walled chancel to greet him, the great reptilian wings unfurling around her, he stood behind one of the columns in the nave, fascinated by her strange deathless beauty. At times her luminous face seemed almost repellent, but he had nonetheless seized on the faint possibility of her resurrection. Each night he came, stealing into the tomb where she had lain for ten thousand years, unable to bring himself to interrupt her. The long copper hair streamed behind her like an entrained time-wind, her angled body in flight between two infinitely distant universes, where archetypal beings of superhuman stature glimmered fitfully in their own self-generated light.

Two days later Bridges discovered the remainder of the drums.

'Traxel! Traxel!' he bellowed, racing across the inner courtyard from the entrance to one of the disused bunkers. He bounded into the ballroom and slammed the metal cans on to the computer which Traxel was programming. 'Take a look at these – more Tenths! The whole place is crawling with them!'

Traxel weighed the cans idly in his hands, glancing across at Shepley and the Old Man, on lookout duty by the window. 'Interesting. Where did you find them?'

Shepley jumped down from the window trestle. 'They're mine. The Doctor will confirm it. They run in sequence after the first I gave you a week ago. I was storing them.'

Bridges cut back with an oath. 'Whaddya mean, storing them? Is that your personal bunker out there? Since when?' He shoved Shepley away with a broad hand and swung round on Traxel. 'Listen, Traxel, those tapes were a fair find. I don't see any tags on them. Every time I bring something in I'm going to have this kid claim it?'

Traxel stood up, adjusting his height so that he overreached Bridges. 'Of course, you're right – technically. But we have to work together, don't we? Shepley made a mistake, we'll forgive him this time.' He handed the drums to Shepley, Bridges seething with barely controlled indignation. 'If I were you, Shepley, I'd get those cashed. Don't worry about flooding the market.' As Shepley turned away, sidestepping Bridges, he called him back. 'And there are advantages in working together, you know.'

He watched Shepley disappear to his room, then turned to survey the huge peeling map of the sand-sea that covered the facing wall.

'You'll have to strip the tombs now,' the Old Man told Shepley later. 'It's obvious you've stumbled on something, and it won't take Traxel five minutes to discover where.'

'Perhaps a little longer,' Shepley replied evenly. They stepped out of the shadow of the palace and moved away among the dunes; Bridges and Traxel were watching them from the dining-room table, their figures motionless in the light. 'The roofs are almost completely covered now. The next sandstorm should bury them for good.'

'Have you entered any of the other tombs?'

Shepley shook his head vigorously. 'Believe me, Doctor, I know now why the time-wardens are here. As long as there's a chance of their being resurrected we're committing murder every time we rob a tomb. Even if it's only one chance in a million it may be all they themselves bargained on. After all, one doesn't commit suicide because the chances of life existing anywhere are virtually nil.'

Already he had come to believe that the enchantress might

suddenly resurrect herself, step down from the catafalque before his eyes. While a slender possibility existed of her returning to life he felt that he too had a valid foothold in existence, that there was a small element of certainty in what had previously seemed a random and utterly meaningless universe.

IV

As the first dawn light probed through the casements, Shepley turned reluctantly from the nave. He looked back briefly at the glowing persona, suppressing the slight pang of disappointment that the expected metamorphosis had not yet occurred, but relieved to have spent as much time awaiting it as possible

He made his way down to the old cantonment, steering carefully through the shadows. As he reached the mono-rail – he now made the journey on foot, to prevent Traxel guessing that the cache lay along the route of the rail – he heard the track hum faintly in the cool air. He jumped back behind a low mound, tracing its winding pathway through the dunes.

Suddenly an engine throbbed out behind him, and Traxel's camouflaged half-track appeared over the edge of the ridge. Its front four wheels raced and spun, and the huge vehicle tipped forward and plunged down the incline among the buried tombs, its surging tracks dislodging tons of the fine sand Shepley had so laboriously pushed by hand up the slope. Immediately several of the pavilions appeared to view, the white dust cascading off their cupolas.

Half-buried in the avalanche they had set off, Traxel and Bridges leapt from the driving cab, pointing to the pavilions and shouting at each other. Shepley darted forward, and put his foot up on the mono-rail just as it began to vibrate loudly.

In the distance the gyro-car slowly approached, the Old Man punting it along, hatless and dishevelled.

He reached the tomb as Bridges was kicking the door in with a heavy boot, Traxel behind him with a bag full of wrenches.

'Hello, Shepley!' Traxel greeted him gaily. 'So this is your treasure trove.'

Shepley staggered splay-legged through the sliding sand, and brushed past Traxel as glass spattered from the window. He flung himself on Bridges and pulled the big man backwards.

'Bridges, this one's mine! Try any of the others; you can have them all!'

Bridges jerked himself to his feet, staring down angrily at Shepley. Traxel peered suspiciously at the other tombs, their porticos still flooded with sand. 'What's so interesting about this one, Shepley?' he asked sardonically. Bridges roared and slammed a boot into the casement, knocking out one of the panels. Shepley dived on to his shoulders, and Bridges snarled and flung him against the wall. Before Shepley could duck he swung a heavy left cross to Shepley's mouth, knocking him back on to the sand with a bloody face.

Traxel roared with amusement as Shepley lay there stunned, then knelt down, sympathetically examining Shepley's face in the light thrown by the expanding persona within the tomb. Bridges whooped with surprise, gaping like a startled ape at the sumptuous golden mirage of the enchantress.

'How did you find me?' Shepley muttered thickly. 'I double-tracked a dozen times.'

Traxel smiled. 'We didn't follow you, chum. We followed the rail.' He pointed down at the silver thread of the metal strip, plainly visible in the dawn light almost ten miles away. 'The gyro-car cleaned the rail. It led us straight here. Ah, hello, Doctor,' he greeted the Old Man as he climbed the slope and slumped down wearily beside Shepley. 'I take it we have you to thank for this discovery. Don't worry, Doctor, I shan't forget you.'

'Many thanks,' the Old Man said flatly. He helped Shepley to sit up, frowning at his split lips. 'Aren't you taking everything too seriously, Traxel? You're becoming crazed with greed. Let the boy have this tomb. There are plenty more.'

The patterns of light across the sand dimmed and broke as Bridges plunged through the persona towards the rear of the chancel. Weakly Shepley tried to stand up, but the Old Man held him back. Traxel shrugged. 'Too late, Doctor.' He looked over his shoulder at the persona, ruefully shaking his head in acknowledgment of its magnificence. 'These 10th Dynasty graves are stupendous. But there's something curious about this one.'

He was still staring at it reflectively a minute later when Bridges emerged.

'Boy, that was a crazy one, Traxel! For a second I thought it was a dud.' He handed the three canisters to Traxel, who weighed two of them in one hand against the other. Bridges added 'Kinda light, aren't they?'

Traxel began to pry them open with a wrench. 'Are you certain there are no more in there?'

'Hundred per cent. Have a look yourself.'

Two of the cans were empty, the tape spools missing. The third was only half full, a mere three-inch width of tape in its centre. Bridges bellowed in pain: 'The kid robbed us. I can't believe it!' Traxel waved him away and went over to the Old Man, who was staring in at the now flickering persona. The two men exchanged glances, then nodded slowly in confirmation. With a short laugh Traxel kicked at the can containing the half reel of tape, jerking the spool out on to the sand, where it began to unravel in the quietly moving air. Bridges protested but Traxel shook his head.

'It *is* a dud. Go and have a close look at the image.' When Bridges peered at it blankly he explained 'The woman there was dead when the matrices were recorded. She's beautiful all right – as poor Shepley here discovered – but it's all too literally skin deep. That's why there's only half a can of data. No nervous system, no musculature or internal organs – just a beautiful golden husk. This is a mortuary tomb. If you resurrected her you'd have an ice-cold corpse on your hands.'

'But why?' Bridges rasped. 'What's the point?'

Traxel gestured expansively. 'It's immortality of a kind. Perhaps she died suddenly, and this was the next best thing. When the Doctor first came here there were a lot of mortuary tombs of young children being found. If I remember he had something of a reputation for always leaving them intact. A typical piece of highbrow sentimentality – giving immortality only to the dead. Agree, Doctor?'

Before the Old Man could reply a voice shouted from below, there was a nearby roaring hiss of an ascending signal rocket and a vivid red star-shell burst over the lake below, spitting incandescent fragments over them. Traxel and Bridges leapt forwards, saw two men in a sandcar pointing up at them, and three more vehicles converging across the lake half a mile away.

'The time-wardens!' Traxel shouted. Bridges picked up the tool bag and the two men raced across the slope towards the half-track, the Old Man hobbling after them. He turned back to wait for Shepley, who was still sitting on the ground where he had fallen, watching the image inside the pavilion.

'Shepley! Come on, lad, pull yourself together! You'll get ten years!'

When Shepley made no reply he reached up to the side of the half-track as Traxel reversed it expertly out of the morraine of sand, letting Bridges swing him aboard. 'Shepley!' he called again. Traxel hesitated, then roared away as a second star-shell exploded.

Shepley tried to reach the tape, but the stampeding feet had severed it at several points, and the loose ends, which he had numbly thought of trying to reinsert into the projector, now fluttered around him in the sand. Below, he could hear the sounds of flight and pursuit, the warning crack of a rifle, engines baying and plunging, as Traxel eluded the time-wardens, but he kept his eyes fixed on the image within the tomb. Already it had begun to fragment, fading against the mounting sunlight. Getting slowly to his feet, he entered the tomb and closed the battered doors.

Still magnificent upon her bier, the enchantress lay back between the great wings. Motionless for so long, she had at last been galvanized into life, and a jerking syncopated rhythm rippled through her body. The wings shook uneasily, and a series of tremors disturbed the base of the catafalque, so that the woman's feet danced an exquisitely flickering minuet, the toes darting from side to side with untiring speed. Higher up, her wide smooth hips jostled each other in a jaunty mock tango.

He watched until only the face remained, a few disconnected traces of the wings and catafalque jerking faintly in the darkness, then made his way out of the tomb.

Outside, in the cool morning light, the time-wardens were waiting for him, hands on the hips of their white uniforms. One was holding the empty canisters, turning the fluttering strands of tape over with his foot as they drifted away.

The other took Shepley's arm and steered him down to the car.

'Traxel's gang,' he said to the driver. 'This must be a new recruit.' He glanced dourly at the blood around Shepley's mouth. 'Looks as if they've been fighting over the spoils.'

The driver pointed to the three drums. 'Stripped?'

The man carrying them nodded. 'All three. And they were 10th

33

Dynasty.' He shackled Shepley's wrists to the dashboard. 'Too bad, son, you'll be doing ten yourself soon. It'll seem like ten thousand.'

'Unless it was a dud,' the driver rejoined, eyeing Shepley with some sympathy. 'You know, one of those freak mortuary tombs.'

Shepley straightened his bruised mouth. 'It wasn't,' he said firmly.

The driver glanced warningly at the other wardens. 'What about the tape blowing away up there?'

Shepley looked up at the tomb spluttering faintly below the ridge, its light almost gone. 'That's just the persona,' he said. 'The empty skin.'

As the engine surged forward he listened to three empty drums hit the floor behind the seat.

Track 12

'Guess again,' Sheringham said.

Maxted clipped on the headphones, carefully settled them over his ears. He concentrated as the disc began to spin, trying to catch some echo of identity.

The sound was a rapid metallic rustling, like iron filings splashing through a funnel. It ran for ten seconds, repeated itself a dozen times, then ended abruptly in a string of blips.

'Well?' Sheringham asked. 'What is it?'

Maxted pulled off his headphones, rubbed one of his ears. He had been listening to the records for hours and his ears felt bruised and numb.

'Could be anything. An ice-cube melting?'

Sheringham shook his head, his little beard wagging.

Maxted shrugged. 'A couple of galaxies colliding?'

'No. Sound waves don't travel through space. I'll give you a clue. It's one of those *proverbial* sounds.' He seemed to be enjoying the catechism.

Maxted lit a cigarette, threw the match onto the laboratory bench. The head melted a tiny pool of wax, froze and left a shallow black scar. He watched it pleasurably, conscious of Sheringham fidgeting beside him.

He pumped his brains for an obscene simile. 'What about a fly – '

'Time's up,' Sheringham cut in. '*A pin dropping.*' He took the 3-inch disc off the player, angled it into its sleeve.

'In actual fall, that is, not impact. We used a fifty-foot shaft and eight microphones. I thought you'd get that one.'

He reached for the last record, a 12-inch LP, but Maxted stood up before he got it to the turntable. Through the french windows he could see the patio, a table, glasses and decanter gleaming in the darkness. Sheringham and his infantile games suddenly irritated him; he felt impatient with himself for tolerating the man so long.

'Let's get some air,' he said brusquely, shouldering past one of the amplifier rigs. 'My ears feel like gongs.'

'By all means' Sheringham agreed promptly. He placed the record carefully on the turntable and switched off the player. 'I want to save this one until later anyway.'

They went out into the warm evening air. Sheringham turned on the Japanese lanterns and they stretched back in the wicker chairs under the open sky.

'I hope you weren't too bored,' Sheringham said as he handled the decanter. 'Microsonics is a fascinating hobby, but I'm afraid I may have let it become an obsession.'

Maxted grunted non-committally. 'Some of the records are interesting,' he admitted. 'They have a sort of crazy novelty value, like blown-up photographs of moths' faces and razor blades. Despite what you claim, though, I can't believe microsonics will ever become a scientific tool. It's just an elaborate laboratory toy.'

Sheringham shook his head. 'You're completely wrong, of course. Remember the cell division series I played first of all? Amplified 100,000 times animal cell division sounds like a lot of girders and steel sheets being ripped apart – how did you put it? – a car smash in slow motion. On the other hand, plant cell division is an electronic poem, all soft chords and bubbling tones. Now there you have a perfect illustration of how microsonics can reveal the distinction between the animal and plant kingdoms.'

'Seems a damned roundabout way of doing it,' Maxted commented, helping himself to soda. 'You might as well calculate the speed of your car from the apparent motion of the stars. Possible, but it's easier to look at the speedometer.'

Sheringham nodded, watching Maxted closely across the table. His interest in the conversation appeared to have exhausted itself, and the two men sat silently with their glasses. Strangely, the hostility between them, of so many years' standing, now became less veiled, the contrast of personality, manner and physique more pronounced. Maxted, a tall fleshy man with a coarse handsome face, lounged back almost horizontally in his chair, thinking about Susan Sheringham. She was at the Turnbulls' party, and but for the fact that it was no longer discreet of him to be seen at the Turnbulls' – for the all-too-familiar reason – he would have passed the evening with her, rather than with her grotesque little husband.

He surveyed Sheringham with as much detachment as he could muster, wondering whether this prim unattractive man, with his pedantry and in-bred academic humour, had any redeeming qualities whatever. None, certainly, at a casual glance, though it required some courage and pride to have invited him round that evening. His motives, however, would be typically eccentric.

The pretext, Maxted reflected, had been slight enough – Sheringham, professor of biochemistry at the university, maintained a lavish home laboratory; Maxted, a run-down athlete with a bad degree, acted as torpedo-man for a company manufacturing electron microscopes; a visit, Sheringham had suggested over the phone, might be to the profit of both.

Of course, nothing of this had in fact been mentioned. But nor, as yet, had he referred to Susan, the real subject of the evening's charade. Maxted speculated upon the possible routes Sheringham might take towards the inevitable confrontation scene; not for him the nervous circular pacing, the well-thumbed photostat, or the tug at the shoulder. There was a vicious adolescent streak running through Sheringham –

Maxted broke out of his reverie abruptly. The air in the patio had become suddenly cooler, almost as if a powerful refrigerating unit had been switched on. A rash of goose-flesh raced up his thighs and down the back of his neck, and he reached forward and finished what was left of his whisky.

'Cold out here,' he commented.

Sheringham glanced at his watch. 'Is it?' he said. There was a hint of indecision in his voice; for a moment he seemed to be waiting for a signal. Then he pulled himself together and, with an odd half-smile, said: 'Time for the last record.'

'What do you mean?' Maxted asked.

'Don't move,' Sheringham said. He stood up. 'I'll put it on.' He pointed to a loudspeaker screwed to the wall above Maxted's head, grinned and ducked out.

Shivering uncomfortably, Maxted peered up into the silent evening sky, hoping that the vertical current of cold air that had sliced down into the patio would soon dissipate itself.

A low noise crackled from the speaker, multiplied by a circle of other speakers which he noticed for the first time had been slung among the trellis-work around the patio.

Shaking his head sadly at Sheringham's antics, he decided to help himself to more whisky. As he stretched across the table he swayed and rolled back uncontrollably into his chair. His stomach seemed to be full of mercury, ice-cold and enormously heavy. He pushed

37

himself forward again, trying to reach the glass, and knocked it across the table. His brain began to fade, and he leaned his elbows helplessly on the glass edge of the table and felt his head fall onto his wrists.

When he looked up again Sheringham was standing in front of him, smiling sympathetically.

'Not too good, eh? ' he said.

Breathing with difficulty, Maxted managed to lean back. He tried to speak to Sheringham, but he could no longer remember any words. His heart switchbacked, and he grimaced at the pain.

'Don't worry,' Sheringham assured him. 'The fibrillation is only a side effect. Disconcerting, perhaps, but it will soon pass.'

He strolled leisurely around the patio, scrutinizing Maxted from several angles. Evidently satisfied, he sat down on the table. He picked up the siphon and swirled the contents about. 'Chromium cyanate. Inhibits the coenzyme system controlling the body's fluid balances, floods hydroxyl ions into the bloodstream. In brief, you drown. Really drown, that is, not merely suffocate as you would if you were immersed in an external bath. However, I mustn't distract you.'

He inclined his head at the speakers. Being fed into the patio was a curiously muffled spongy noise, like elastic waves lapping in a latex sea. The rhythms were huge and ungainly, overlayed by the deep leaden wheezing of a gigantic bellows. Barely audible at first, the sounds rose until they filled the patio and shut out the few traffic noises along the highway.

'Fantastic, isn't it?' Sheringham said. Twirling the siphon by its neck he stepped over Maxted's legs and adjusted the tone control under one of the speaker boxes. He looked blithe and spruce, almost ten years younger. 'These are 30-second repeats, 400 microsens, amplification one thousand. I admit I've edited the track a little, but it's still remarkable how repulsive a beautiful sound can become. You'll never guess what this was.'

Maxted stirred sluggishly. The lake of mercury in his stomach was as cold and bottomless as an oceanic trench, and his arms and legs had become enormous, like the bloated appendages of a drowned giant. He could just see Sheringham bobbing about in front of him, and hear the slow beating of the sea in the distance. Nearer now, it pounded with a dull insistent rhythm, the great waves ballooning and bursting like bubbles in a lava sea.

'I'll tell you, Maxted, it took me a year to get that recording,'

Sheringham was saying. He straddled Maxted, gesturing with the siphon. 'A year. Do you know how ugly a year can be?' For a moment he paused, then tore himself from the memory. 'Last Saturday, just after midnight, you and Susan were lying back in this same chair. You know, Maxted, there are audio-probes everywhere here. Slim as pencils, with a six-inch focus. I had four in that headrest alone.' He added, as a footnote: 'The wind is your own breathing, fairly heavy at the time, if I remember; your interlocked pulses produced the thunder effect.'

Maxted drifted in a wash of sound.

Some while later Sheringham's face filled his eyes, beard wagging, mouth working wildly.

'Maxted! You've only two more guesses, so for God's sake concentrate,' he shouted irritably, his voice almost lost among the thunder rolling from the sea. 'Come on, man, what is it? Maxted!' he bellowed. He leapt for the nearest loudspeaker and drove up the volume. The sound boomed out of the patio, reverberating into the night.

Maxted had almost gone now, his fading identity a small feature-less island nearly eroded by the waves beating across it.

Sheringham knelt down and shouted into his ear.

'Maxted, can you hear the sea? Do you know where you're drowning?'

A succession of gigantic flaccid waves, each more lumbering and enveloping than the last, rode down upon them.

'In a kiss!' Sheringham screamed. 'A kiss!'

The island slipped and slid away into the molten shelf of the sea.

Passport to Eternity

It was half past love on New Day in Zenith and the clocks were striking heaven. All over the city the sounds of revelry echoed upwards into the dazzling Martian night, but high on Sunset Ridge, among the mansions of the rich, Margot and Clifford Gorrell faced each other in glum silence.

Frowning, Margot flipped impatiently through the vacation brochure on her lap, then tossed it away with an elaborate gesture of despair.

'But Clifford, why do we have to go to the same place every summer? I'd like to do something interesting for a change. This year the Lovatts are going to the Venus Fashion Festival, and Bobo and Peter Anders have just booked into the fire beaches at Saturn. They'll all have a wonderful time, while we're quietly taking the last boat to nowhere.'

Clifford Gorrell nodded impassively, one hand cupped over the sound control in the arm of his chair. They had been arguing all evening, and Margot's voice threw vivid sparks of irritation across the walls and ceiling. Grey and mottled, they would take days to drain.

'I'm sorry you feel like that, Margot. Where would you like to go?'

Margot shrugged scornfully, staring out at the corona of a million neon signs that illuminated the city below. 'Does it matter?'

'Of course. You arrange the vacation this time.'

Margot hesitated, one eye keenly on her husband. Then she sat forward happily, turning up her fluorescent violet dress until she glowed like an Algolian rayfish.

'Clifford, I've got a wonderful idea! Yesterday I was down in the Colonial Bazaar, thinking about our holiday, when I found a small dream bureau that's just been opened. Something like the Dream Dromes in Neptune City everyone was crazy about two or three years ago, but instead of having to plug into whatever programme happens to be going you have your own dream plays specially designed for you.'

Clifford continued to nod, carefully increasing the volume of the sound-sweeper.

'They have their own studios and send along a team of analysts and writers to interview us and afterwards book a sanatorium anywhere we like for the convalescence. Eve Corbusier and I decided a small party of five or six would be best.'

'Eve Corbusier,' Clifford repeated. He smiled thinly to himself and switched on the book he had been reading. 'I wondered when that Gorgon was going to appear.'

'Eve isn't too bad when you get to know her, darling,' Margot told him. 'Don't start reading yet. She'll think up all sorts of weird ideas for the play.' Her voice trailed off. 'What's the matter?'

'Nothing,' Clifford said wearily. 'It's just that I sometimes wonder if you have any sense of responsibility at all.' As Margot's eyes darkened he went on. 'Do you really think that I, a supreme court justice, could take that sort of vacation, even if I wanted to? Those dream plays are packed with advertising commercials and all sorts of corrupt material.' He shook his head sadly. 'And I told you not to go into the Colonial Bazaar.'

'What are we going to do then?' Margot asked coldly. 'Another honeyMoon?'

'I'll reserve a couple of singles tomorrow. Don't worry, you'll enjoy it.' He clipped the hand microphone into his book and began to scan the pages with it, listening to the small metallic voice.

Margot stood up, the vanes in her hat quivering furiously. 'Clifford!' she snapped, her voice dead and menacing. 'I warn you, I'm not going on another honeyMoon!'

Absently, Clifford said: 'Of course, dear,' his fingers racing over the volume control.

'Clifford!'

Her shout sank to an angry squeak. She stepped over to him, her dress blazing like a dragon, jabbering at him noiselessly, the sounds sucked away through the vents over her head and pumped out across the echoing rooftops of the midnight city.

As he sat back quietly in his private vacuum, the ceiling shaking occasionally when Margot slammed a door upstairs, Clifford looked out over the brilliant diadem of down-town Zenith. In the distance, by the space-port, the ascending arcs of hyperliners flared across the sky while below the countless phosphorescent trajectories of hop-cabs enclosed the bowl of rooflight in a dome of glistening hoops.

Of all the cities of the galaxy, few offered such a wealth of pleasures as Zenith, but to Clifford Gorrell it was as distant and unknown as the first Gomorrah. At 35 he was a thin-faced, prematurely ageing man with receding hair and a remote abstracted expression, and in the dark sombre suit and stiff white dog-collar which were the traditional uniform of the Probate Department's senior administrators he looked like a man who had never taken a holiday in his life.

At that moment Clifford wished he hadn't. He and Margot had never been able to agree about their vacations. Clifford's associates and superiors at the Department, all of them ten or twenty years older than himself, took their pleasures conservatively and expected a young but responsible justice to do the same. Margot grudgingly acknowledged this, but her friends who frequented the chic playtime clinics along the beach at Mira Mira considered the so-called honeyMoon trips back to Earth derisively old-fashioned, a last desperate resort of the aged and infirm.

And to tell the truth, Clifford realized, they were right. He had never dared to admit to Margot that he too was bored because it would have been more than his peace of mind was worth, but a change might do them good.

He resolved – next year.

Margot lay back among the cushions on the terrace divan, listening to the flamingo trees singing to each other in the morning sunlight. Twenty feet below, in the high-walled garden, a tall muscular young man was playing with a jet-ball. He had a dark olive complexion and swarthy good looks, and oil gleamed across his bare chest and arms. Margot watched with malicious amusement his efforts to entertain her. This was Trantino, Margot's play-boy, who chaperoned her during Clifford's long absences at the Probate Department.

'Hey, Margot! Catch!' He gestured with the jet-ball but Margot turned away, feeling her swim-suit slide pleasantly across her smooth tanned skin. The suit was made of one of the newer bioplastic materials, and its living tissues were still growing, softly adapting themselves to the contours of her body, repairing themselves as the fibres became worn or grimy. Upstairs in her wardrobes the gowns and dresses purred on their hangers like the drowsing inmates of some exquisite arboreal zoo. Sometimes she thought of commissioning her little Mercurian tailor to run up a bioplastic suit for Clifford – a specially designed suit that would begin to constrict one night as he stood on the terrace, the lapels growing tighter and tighter around his neck, the sleeves pinning his arms to his sides, the waist contracting to pitch him over –

'Margot!' Trantino interrupted her reverie, sailed the jet-ball expertly through the air towards her. Annoyed, Margot caught it with one hand and pointed it away, watched it sail over the wall and the roofs beyond.

Trantino came up to her. 'What's the matter?' he asked anxiously. For his part he felt his inability to soothe Margot a reflection on his professional skill. The privileges of his caste had to be guarded jealously. For several centuries now the managerial and technocratic elite had been so preoccupied with the work of government that they relied on the Templars of Aphrodite not merely to guard their wives from any marauding suitors but also to keep them amused and contented. By definition, of course, their relationship was platonic, a pleasant revival of the old chivalrous ideals, but sometimes Trantino regretted that the only tools in his armoury were a handful of poems and empty romantic gestures. The Guild of which he was a novitiate member was an ancient and honoured one, and it wouldn't do if Margot began to pine and Mr Gorrell reported him to the Masters of the Guild.

'Why are you always arguing with Mr Gorrell?' Trantino asked her. One of the Guild's axioms was 'The husband *is always* right.' Any discord between him and his wife was the responsibility of the play-boy.

Margot ignored Trantino's question. 'Those trees are getting on my nerves,' she complained fractiously. 'Why can't they keep quiet?'

'They're mating,' Trantino told her. He added thoughtfully: 'You should sing to Mr Gorrell.'

Margot stirred lazily as the shoulder straps of the sun-suit unclasped themselves behind her back. 'Tino,' she asked, 'What's the most unpleasant thing I could do to Mr Gorrell?'

'Margot!' Trantino gasped, utterly shocked. He decided that an appeal to sentiment, a method of reconciliation despised by the more proficient members of the Guild, was his only hope. 'Remember, Margot, you will always have me.'

43

He was about to permit himself a melancholy smile when Margot sat up abruptly.

'Don't look so frightened, you fool! I've just got an idea that should make Mr Gorrell sing to me.'

She straightened the vanes in her hat, waited for the sunsuit to clasp itself discreetly around her, then pushed Trantino aside and stalked off the terrace.

Clifford was browsing among the spools in the library, quietly listening to an old 22nd Century abstract on systems of land tenure in the Trianguli.

'Hello, Margot, feel better now?'

Margot smiled at him coyly. 'Clifford, I'm ashamed of myself. Do forgive me.' She bent down and nuzzled his ear. 'Sometimes I'm very selfish. Have you booked our tickets yet?'

Clifford disengaged her arm and straightened his collar. 'I called the agency, but their bookings have been pretty heavy. They've got a double but no singles. We'll have to wait a few days.'

'No, we won't,' Margot exclaimed brightly. 'Clifford, why don't you and I take the double? Then we can really be together, forget all that ship-board nonsense about never having met before.'

Puzzled, Clifford switched off the player. 'What do you mean?'

Margot explained. 'Look, Clifford, I've been thinking that I ought to spend more time with you than I do at present, really share your work and hobbies. I'm tired of all these play-boys.' She drooped languidly against Clifford, her voice silky and reassuring. 'I want to be with you, Clifford. *Always.*'

Clifford pushed her away. 'Don't be silly, Margot,' he said with an anxious laugh. 'You're being absurd.'

'No, I'm not. After all, Harold Kharkov and his wife haven't got a play-boy and she's very happy.'

Maybe she is, Clifford thought, beginning to panic. Kharkov had once been the powerful and ruthless director of the Department of Justice, now was a third-rate attorney hopelessly trying to eke out a meagre living on the open market, dominated by his wife and forced to spend virtually 24 hours a day with her. For a moment Clifford thought of the days when he had courted Margot, of the long dreadful hours listening to her inane chatter. Trantino's real role was not to chaperone Margot while Clifford was away but while he was at home.

'Margot, be sensible,' he started to say, but she cut him short.

44

'I've made up my mind, I'm going to tell Trantino to pack his suitcase and go back to the Guild.' She switched on the spool player, selecting the wrong speed, smiling ecstatically as the reading head grated loudly and stripped the coding off the record. 'It's going to be wonderful to share everything with you. Why don't we forget about the vacation this year?'

A facial tic from which Clifford had last suffered at the age of ten began to twitch ominously.

Tony Harcourt, Clifford's personal assistant, came over to the Gorrell's villa immediately after lunch. He was a brisk, polished young man, barely controlling his annoyance at being called back to work on the first day of his vacation. He had carefully booked a sleeper next to Dolores Costane, the most beautiful of the Jovian Heresiarch's vestals, on board a leisure-liner leaving that afternoon for Venus, but instead of enjoying the fruits of weeks of blackmail and intrigue he was having to take part in what seemed a quite uncharacteristic piece of Gorrell whimsy.

He listened in growing bewilderment as Clifford explained.

'We were going to one of our usual resorts on Luna, Tony, but we've decided we need a change. Margot wants a vacation that's different. Something new, exciting, original. So go round all the agencies and bring me their suggestions.'

'All the agencies?' Tony queried. 'Don't you mean just the registered ones?'

'All of them,' Margot told him smugly, relishing every moment of her triumph.

Clifford nodded, and smiled at Margot benignly.

'But there must be 50 or 60 agencies organizing vacations,' Tony protested. 'Only about a dozen of them are accredited. Outside Empyrean Tours and Union-Galactic there'll be absolutely nothing suitable for you.'

'Never mind,' Clifford said blandly. 'We only want an idea of the field. I'm sorry, Tony, but I don't want this all over the Department and I know you'll be discreet.'

Tony groaned. 'It'll take me weeks.'

'Three days,' Clifford told him. 'Margot and I want to leave here by the end of the week.' He looked longingly over his shoulder for the absent Trantino. 'Believe me, Tony, we really need a holiday.'

* * *

Fifty-six travel and vacation agencies were listed in the Commercial Directory, Tony discovered when he returned to his office in the top floor of the Justice building in downtown Zenith, all but eight of them alien. The Department had initiated legal proceedings against five, three had closed down, and eight more were fronts for other enterprises.

That left him with forty to visit, spread all over the Upper and Lower Cities and in the Colonial Bazaar, attached to various mercantile, religious and paramilitary organizations, some of them huge concerns with their own police and ecclesiastical forces, others sharing a one-room office and transceiver with a couple of other shoestring firms.

Tony mapped out an itinerary, slipped a flask of Five-Anchor Neptunian Rum into his hip pocket and dialled a helicab.

The first was ARCO PRODUCTIONS INC., a large establishment occupying three levels and a bunker on the fashionable west side of the Upper City. According to the Directory they specialized in hunting and shooting expeditions.

The helicab put him down on the apron outside the entrance. Massive steel columns reached up to a reinforced concrete portico, and the whole place looked less like a travel agency than the last redoubt of some interstellar Seigfreid. As he went in a smart jackbooted guard of janissaries in black and silver uniforms snapped to attention and presented arms.

Everyone inside the building was wearing a uniform, moving about busily at standby alert. A huge broad-shouldered woman with sergeant's stripes handed Tony over to a hard-faced Martian colonel.

'I'm making some inquiries on behalf of a wealthy Terran and his wife,' Tony explained. 'They thought they'd do a little big-game hunting on their vacation this year. I believe you organize expeditions.'

The colonel nodded curtly and led Tony over to a broad map-table. 'Certainly. What exactly have they in mind?'

'Well, nothing really. They hoped you'd make some suggestions.'

'Of course.' The colonel pulled out a memo-tape. 'Have they their own air and land forces?'

Tony shook his head. 'I'm afraid not.'

'I see. Can you tell me whether they will require a single army corps, a combined task force or – '

'No,' Tony said. 'Nothing as big as that.'

'An assault party of brigade strength? I understand. Quieter and less elaborate. All the fashion today.' He switched on the star-map and spread his hands across the glimmering screen of stars and nebulae. 'Now the question of the particular theatre. At present only three of the game reserves have open seasons. Firstly the Procyon system; this includes about 20 different races, some of them still with only atomic technologies. Unfortunately there's been a good deal of dispute recently about declaring Procyon a game reserve, and the Resident of Alschain is trying to have it admitted to the Pan-Galactic Conference. A pity, I feel,' the colonel added, reflectively stroking his steel-grey moustache. 'Procyon always put up a great fight against us and an expedition there was invariably lively.'

Tony nodded sympathetically. 'I hadn't realized they objected.'

The colonel glanced at him sharply. 'Naturally,' he said. He cleared his throat. 'That leaves only the Ketab tribes of Ursa Major, who are having their Millennial Wars, and the Sudor Martines of Orion. They are an entirely new reserve, and your best choice without doubt. The ruling dynasty died out recently, and a war of succession could be conveniently arranged.'

Tony was no longer following the colonel, but he smiled intelligently.

'Now,' the colonel asked, 'what political or spiritual creeds do your friends wish to have invoked?'

Tony frowned. 'I don't think they want any. Are they absolutely necessary?'

The colonel regarded Tony carefully. 'No,' he said slowly. 'It's a question of taste. A purely military operation is perfectly feasible. However, we always advise our clients to invoke some doctrine as a *casus belli*, not only to avoid adverse publicity and any feelings of guilt or remorse, but to lend colour and purpose to the campaign. Each of our field commanders specializes in a particular ideological pogrom, with the exception of General Westerling. Perhaps your friends would prefer him?'

Tony's mind started to work again. 'Schapiro Westerling? The former Director-General of Graves Commission?'

The colonel nodded. 'You know him?'

Tony laughed. 'Know him? I thought I was prosecuting him at the current Nova Trials. I can see that we're well behind with the times.'

He pushed back his chair. 'To tell the truth I don't think you've anything suitable for my friends. Thanks all the same.'

The colonel stiffened. One of his hands moved below the desk and a buzzer sounded along the wall.

'However,' Tony added, 'I'd be grateful if you'd send them further details.'

The colonel sat impassively in his chair. Three enormous guards appeared at Tony's elbow, idly swinging energy truncheons.

'Clifford Gorrell, Stellar Probate Division, Department of Justice,' Tony said quickly.

He gave the colonel a brief smile and made his way out, cursing Clifford and walking warily across the thickly-piled carpet in case it had been mined.

The next one on his list was the A-Z JOLLY JUBILEE COMPANY, alien and unregistered, head office somewhere out of Betelgeuse. According to the Directory they specialized in 'all-in cultural parties and guaranteed somatic week-ends.' Their premises occupied the top two tiers of a hanging garden in the Colonial Bazaar. They sounded harmless enough but Tony was ready for them.

'No,' he said firmly to a lovely Antarean wraith-fern who shyly raised a frond to him as he crossed the terrace. 'Not today.'

Behind the bar a fat man in an asbestos suit was feeding sand to a siliconic fire-fish swimming round in a pressure brazier.

'Damn things,' he grumbled, wiping the sweat off his chin and fiddling aimlessly with the thermostat. 'They gave me a booklet when I got it, but it doesn't say anything about it eating a whole beach every day.' He spaded in another couple of shovels from a low dune of sand heaped on the floor behind him. 'You have to keep them at exactly 5750°K. or they start getting nervous. Can I help you?'

'I thought there was a vacation agency here,' Tony said.

'Sure. I'll call the girls for you.' He pressed a bell.

'Wait a minute,' Tony cut in. 'You advertise something about cultural parties. What exactly are they?'

The fat man chuckled. 'That must be my partner. He's a professor at Vega Tech. Likes to keep the tone up.' He winked at Tony.

Tony sat on one of the stools, looking out over the crazy spiral roof-tops of the Bazaar. A mile away the police patrols circled over the big apartment batteries which marked the perimeter of the Bazaar, keeping their distance.

A tall slim woman appeared from behind the foliage and sauntered across the terrace to him. She was a Canopan slave, hot-housed out of imported germ, a slender green-skinned beauty with moth-like fluttering gills.

The fat man introduced Tony. 'Lucille, take him up to the arbour and give him a run through.'

Tony tried to protest but the pressure brazier was hissing fiercely. The fat man started feeding sand in furiously, the exhaust flames flaring across the terrace.

Quickly, Tony turned and backed up the stairway to the arbour. 'Lucille,' he reminded her firmly, 'this is strictly cultural, remember.'

Half an hour later a dull boom reverberated up from the terrace.

'Poor Jumbo,' Lucille said sadly as a fine rain of sand came down over them.

'Poor Jumbo,' Tony agreed, sitting back and playing with a coil of her hair. Like a soft sinuous snake, it circled around his arm, sleek with blue oil. He drained the flask of Five-Anchor and tossed it lightly over the balustrade. 'Now tell me more about these Canopan prayerbeds. . .'

When, after two days, Tony reported back to the Gorrells he looked hollow-eyed and exhausted, like a man who had been brain-washed by the Wardens.

'What happened to you?' Margot asked anxiously, 'we thought you'd been going round the agencies.'

'Exactly,' Tony said. He slumped down in a sofa and tossed a thick folder across to Clifford. 'Take your pick. You've got about 250 schemes there in complete detail, but I've written out a synopsis which gives one or two principal suggestions from each agency. Most of them are out of the question.'

Clifford unclipped the synopsis and started to read through it.

(1) ARCO PRODUCTIONS INC. Unregistered. Private subsidiary of Sagittarius Security Police.

Hunting and shooting. Your own war to order. Raiding parties, revolutions, religious crusades. In anything from a small commando squad to a 3,000-ship armada. ARCO provide publicity, mock War Crimes Tribunal, etc. Samples:

(a) Operation Torquemada. 23-day expedition to Bellatrix IV. 20 ship assault corps under Admiral Storm Wengen. Mission: liberation of (imaginary) Terran hostages. Cost: 300,000 credits.

(b) Operation Klingsor. 15-year crusade against Ursa Major. Combined task force of 2,500 ships. Mission: recovery of runic memory dials stolen from client's shrine.

Cost: 500 billion credits (ARCO will arrange lend-lease but this is dabbling in realpolitik).

(2) ARENA FEATURES INC. Unregistered. Organizers of the Pan-Galactic Tournament held tri-millennially at the Sun Bowl 2-Heliopolis, NGC 3599.

Every conceivable game in the Cosmos is played at the tournament and so formidable is the opposition that a winning contestant can virtually choose his own apotheosis. The challenge round of the Solar Megathlon Group 3 (that is, for any being whose function can be described, however loosely, as living) involves Quantum Jumping, 7-dimensional Maze Ball and Psychokinetic Bridge (pretty tricky against a telepathic Ketos D'Oma). The only Terran ever to win an event was the redoubtable Chippy Yerkes of Altair 5 The Clowns, who introduced the unplayable blank Round Dice. Being a spectator is as exhausting as being a contestant, and you're well advised to substitute.

Cost: 100,000 credits/day.

(3) AGENCE GENERALE DE TOURISME. Registered. Venus.

Concessionaires for the Colony Beatific on Lake Virgo, the Mandrake Casino Circuit and the Miramar-Trauma Senso-channels. Dream-baths, vu-dromes, endocrine-galas. Darleen Costello is the current Aphrodite and Laurence Mandell makes a versatile Lothario. Plug into these two from 30:30 VST. Room and non-denominational bath at the Gomorrah-Plaza on Mount Venus comes to 1,000 credits a day, but remember to keep out of the Zone. It's just too erotogenous for a Terran.

(4) TERMINAL TOURS LTD. Unregistered. Earth.

For those who want to get away from it all the *Dream of Osiris*, an astral-rigged, 1,000-foot leisure-liner is now fitting out for the Grand Tour. Round-cosmos cruise, visiting every known race and galaxy.

Cost: Doubles at a flat billion, but it's cheap when you realize that the cruise lasts for ever and you'll never be back.

(5) SLEEP TRADERS. Unregistered.

A somewhat shadowy group who handle all dealings on the Blue Market, acting as a general clearing house and buying and selling dreams all through the Galaxy.

Sample: Like to try a really new sort of dream? The Set Corrani Priests of Theta Piscium will link you up with the sacred electronic thought-pools in the Desert of Kish. These mercury lakes are their ancestral memory banks. Surgery is necessary but be careful. Too much cortical damage and the archetypes may get restive. In return one of the Set Corrani (polysexual delta-humanoids about the size of a walking dragline) will take over your cerebral functions for a long weekend. All these transactions are done on an exchange basis and SLEEP TRADERS charge nothing for the service. But they obviously get a rake-off, and may pump advertising into the lower medullary centres. Whatever they're selling I wouldn't advise anybody to buy.

(6) THE AGENCY. Registered. M33 in Andromeda.

The executive authority of the consortium of banking trusts floating Schedule D, the fourth draw of the gigantic PK pyramid lottery sweeping all through the continuum from Sol III out to the island universes. Trance-cells everywhere are now recruiting dream-readers and ESPerceptionists, and there's still time to buy a ticket. There's only one number on all the tickets – the winning one – but don't think that means you'll get away with the kitty. THE AGENCY has just launched UNILIV, the emergency relief fund for victims of Schedule C who lost their deposits and are now committed to paying off impossible debts, some monetary, some moral (if you're unlucky in the draw you may find yourself landed with a guilt complex that would make even a Colonus Rex look sad).

Cost: 1 credit – but with an evaluation in the billions if you have to forfeit.

(7) ARCTURIAN EXPRESS. Unregistered.

Controls all important track events. The racing calendar this year is a causal and not a temporal one and seems a little obscure, but most of the established classics are taking place.

(8) The Rhinosaur Derby. Held this year at Betelgeuse Springs

51

under the rules of the Federation of Amorphs. First to the light horizon. There's always quite a line-up for this one and any form of vehicle is allowed – rockets, beams, racial migrations, ES thought patterns – but frankly it's a waste of effort. It's not just that by the time you're out of your own sight you're usually out of your mind as well, but the Nils of Rigel, who always enter a strong team, are capable of instantaneous transmission.

(b) The Paraplegic Handicap. Recently instituted by the Protists of Lambda Scorpio. The course measures only 0.00015 mm., but that's a long way to urge an Aldebaran Torpid. They are giant viruses embedded in bauxite mountains, and by varying their pressure differentials it's sometimes possible to tickle them into a little life. K 2 on Regulus IX is holding the big bets, but even so the race is estimated to take about 50,000 years to run.

(8) NEW FUTURES INC. Unregistered.

Tired of the same dull round? NEW FUTURES will take you right out of this world. In the island universes the continuum is extra-dimensional, and the time channels are controlled by rival cartels. The element of chance apparently plays the time role, and it's all even more confused by the fact that you may be moving around in someone else's extrapolation.

In the tourist translation manual 185 basic tenses are given, and of these 125 are future conditional. No verb conjugates in the present tense, and you can invent and copyright your own irregulars. This may explain why I got the impression at the bureau that they were only half there.

Cost: simultaneously 3, 270 and 2,000,000 credits. They refuse to quibble.

(9) SEVEN SIRENS. Registered. Venus.

A subsidiary of the fashion trust controlling senso-channel Astral Eve.

Ladies, like to win your own beauty contest? Twenty-five of the most beautiful creatures in the Galaxy are waiting to pit their charms against yours, but however divine they may be – and two or three of them, such as the Flamen Zilla Quel-Queen (75-9-25) and the Orthodox Virgin of Altair (76-953-?) certainly will be – they'll stand no chance against you. Your specifications will be defined as the ideal ones.

(10) GENERAL ENTERPRISES. Registered.

Specialists in culture cycles, world struggles, ethnic trends. Organize vacations as a sideline. A vast undertaking for whom ultimately we all work. Their next venture, epoch-making by all accounts, is starting now, and everybody will be coming along. I was politely but firmly informed that it was no use worrying about the cost. When I asked –

Before Clifford could finish one of the houseboys came up to him. 'Priority Call for you, sir.'

Clifford handed the synopsis to Margot. 'Tell me if you find anything. It looks to me as if we've been wasting Tony's time.'

He left them and went through to his study.

'Ah, Gorrell, there you are.' It was Thornwall Harrison, the attorney who had taken over Clifford's office. 'Who the hell are all these people trailing in to see you night and day? The place looks like Colonial Night at the Arena Circus. I can't get rid of them.'

'Which people?' Clifford asked. 'What do they want?'

'You apparently,' Thornwall told him. 'Most of them thought I was you. They've been trying to sell me all sorts of crazy vacation schemes. I said you'd already gone on your vacation and I myself never took one. Then one of them pulled a hypodermic on me. There's even an Anti-Cartel agent sleuthing around, wants to see you about block bookings. Thinks you're a racketeer.'

Back in the lounge Margot and Tony were looking out through the terrace windows into the boulevard which ran from the Gorrell's villa to the level below.

A long column of vehicles had pulled up under the trees: trucks, half-tracks, huge Telesenso studio location vans and several sleek white ambulances. The drivers and crew-men were standing about in little groups in the shadows, quietly watching the villa. Two or three radar scanners on the vans were rotating, and as Clifford looked down a convoy of trucks drove up and joined the tail of the column.

'Looks like there's going to be quite a party,' Tony said. 'What are they waiting for?'

'Perhaps they've come for us?' Margot suggested excitedly.

'They're wasting their time if they have,' Clifford told her. He swung round on Tony. 'Did you give our names to any of the agencies?'

53

Tony hesitated, then nodded. 'I couldn't help it. Some of those outfits wouldn't take no for an answer.'

Clifford clamped his lips and picked the synopsis off the floor. 'Well, Margot, have you decided where you want to go?'

Margot fiddled with the synopsis. 'There are so many to choose from.'

Tony started for the door. 'Well, I'll leave you to it.' He waved a hand at them. 'Have fun.'

'Hold on,' Clifford told him. 'Margot hasn't made up her mind yet.'

'What's the hurry?' Tony asked. He indicated the line of vehicles outside, their crews now climbing into their driving cabs and turrets. 'Take your time. You may bite off more than you can chew.'

'Exactly. So as soon as Margot decides where we're going you can make the final arrangements for us and get rid of that menagerie.'

'But Clifford, give me a chance.'

'Sorry. Now Margot, hurry up.'

Margot flipped through the synopsis, screwing up her mouth. 'It's so difficult, Clifford, I don't really like any of these. I still think the best agency was the little one I found in the Bazaar.'

'No,' Tony groaned, sinking down on a sofa. 'Margot, please, after all the trouble I've gone to.'

'Yes, definitely that one. The dream bureau. What was it called – '

Before she could finish there was a roar of engines starting up in the boulevard. Startled, Clifford saw the column of cars and trucks churn across the gravel towards the villa. Music, throbbing heavily, came down from the room above, and a sick musky odour seeped through the air.

Tony pulled himself off the sofa. 'They must have had this place wired,' he said quickly. 'You'd better call the police. Believe me, some of these people don't waste time arguing.'

Outside three helmeted men in brown uniforms ran past the terrace, unwinding a coil of fuse wire. The sharp hissing sound of para-rays sucked through the air from the drive.

Margot hid back in her slumber seat. 'Trantino!' she wailed.

Clifford went back into his study. He switched the transceiver to the emergency channel.

Instead of the police signal a thin automatic voice beeped through. 'Remain seated, remain seated. Take-off in zero two minutes, Purser's office on G Deck now – '

Clifford switched to another channel. There was a blare of studio applause and a loud unctuous voice called out:

'And now over to brilliant young Clifford Gorrell and his charming wife Margot about to enter their dream-pool at the fabulous Riviera-Neptune. Are you there, Cliff?'

Angrily, Clifford turned to a third. Static and morse chattered, and then someone rapped out in a hard iron tone: 'Colonel Sapt is dug in behind the swimming pool. Enfilade along the garage roof – '

Clifford gave up. He went back to the lounge. The music was deafening. Margot was prostrate in her slumber-seat, Tony down on the floor by the window, watching a pitched battle raging in the drive. Heavy black palls of smoke drifted across the terrace, and two tanks with stylized archers emblazoned on their turrets were moving up past the burning wrecks of the studio location vans.

'They must be Arco's!' Tony shouted. 'The police will look after them, but wait until the extra-sensory gang take over!'

Crouching behind a low stone parapet running off the terrace was a group of waiters in dishevelled evening dress, lab technicians in scorched white overalls and musicians clutching their instrument cases. A bolt of flame from one of the tanks flickered over their heads and crashed into the grove of flamingo trees, sending up a shower of sparks and broken notes.

Clifford pulled Tony to his feet. 'Come on, we've got to get out of here. We'll try the library windows into the garden. You'd better take Margot.'

Her yellow beach robe had apparently died of shock, and was beginning to blacken like a dried-out banana skin. Discreetly averting his eyes, Tony picked her up and followed Clifford out into the hall.

Three croupiers in gold uniforms were arguing hotly with two men in white surgeons' coats. Behind them a couple of mechanics were struggling a huge vibrobath up the stairs.

The foreman came over to Clifford. 'Gorrell?' he asked, consulting an invoice. 'Trans-Ocean.' He jerked a thumb at the bath. 'Where do you want it?'

A surgeon elbowed him aside. 'Mr Gorrell?' he asked suavely. 'We are from Cerebro-Tonic Travel. Please allow me to give you a sedative. All this noise – '

Clifford pushed past him and started to walk down the corridor to the library, but the floor began to slide and weave.

55

He stopped and looked around unsteadily.

Tony was down on his knees, Margot flopped out of his arms across the floor.

Someone swayed up to Clifford and held out a tray.

On it were three tickets.

Around him the walls whirled.

He woke in his bedroom, lying comfortably on his back, gently breathing a cool amber air. The noise had died away, but he could still hear a vortex of sound spinning violently in the back of his mind. It spiralled away, vanished, and he moved his head and looked around.

Margot was lying asleep beside him, and for a moment he thought that the attack on the house had been a dream. Then he noticed the skull-plate clamped over his head, and the cables leading off from a boom to a large console at the foot of the bed. Massive spools loaded with magnetic tape waited in the projector ready to be played.

The real nightmare was still to come! He struggled to get up, found himself clamped in a twilight sleep, unable to move more than a few centimetres.

He lay there powerlessly for ten minutes, tongue clogging his mouth like a wad of cotton-wool when he tried to shout. Eventually a small neatly featured alien in a pink silk suit opened the door and padded quietly over to them. He peered down at their faces and then turned a couple of knobs on the console.

Clifford's consciousness began to clear. Beside him Margot stirred and woke.

The alien beamed down pleasantly. 'Good evening,' he greeted them in a smooth creamy voice. 'Please allow me to apologize for any discomfort you have suffered. However, the first day of a vacation is often a little confused.'

Margot sat up. 'I remember you. You're from the little bureau in the Bazaar.' She jumped round happily. 'Clifford!'

The alien bowed. 'Of course, Mrs Gorrell. I am Dr Terence Sotal-2 Burlington, Professor – Emeritus,' he added to himself as an afterthought, '– of Applied Drama at the University of Alpha Leporis, and the director of the play you and your husband are to perform during your vacation.'

Clifford cut in: 'Would you release me from this machine immediately? And then get out of my house! I've had – '

'Clifford!' Margot snapped. 'What's the matter with you?'

Clifford dragged at the skull plate and Dr Burlington quietly moved a control on the console. Part of Clifford's brain clouded and he sank back helplessly.

'Everything is all right, Mr Gorrell,' Dr Burlington said.

'Clifford,' Margot warned him. 'Remember your promise.' She smiled at Dr Burlington. 'Don't pay any attention to him, Doctor. Please go on.'

'Thank you, Mrs Gorrell.' Dr Burlington bowed again, as Clifford lay half-asleep, groaning impotently.

'The play we have designed for you,' Dr Burlington explained, 'is an adaptation of a classic masterpiece in the Diphenyl 2-4-6 Cyclopropane canon, and though based on the oldest of human situations, is nonetheless fascinating. It was recently declared the outright winner at the Mira Nuptial Contest, and will always have a proud place in the private repertoires. To you, I believe, it is known as "The Taming of the Shrew."'

Margot giggled and then looked surprised. Dr Burlington smiled urbanely. 'However, allow me to show you the script.' He excused himself and slipped out.

Margot fretted anxiously, while Clifford pulled weakly at the skull-plate.

'Clifford, I'm not sure that I like this altogether. And Dr Burlington does seem rather strange. But I suppose it's only for three weeks.'

Just then the door opened and a stout bearded figure, erect in a stiff blue uniform, white yachting cap jauntily on his head, stepped in.

'Good evening, Mrs Gorrell.' He saluted Margot smartly, 'Captain Linstrom.' He looked down at Clifford. 'Good to have you aboard, sir.'

'Aboard?' Clifford repeated weakly. He looked around at the familiar furniture in the room, the curtains drawn neatly over the windows. 'What are you raving about? Get out of my house!'

The Captain chuckled. 'Your husband has a sense of humour, Mrs Gorrell. A useful asset on these long trips. Your friend Mr Harcourt in the next cabin seems sadly lacking in one.'

'Tony?' Margot exclaimed. 'Is he still here?'

Captain Linstrom laughed. 'I quite understand you. He seems

very worried, quite over-eager to return to Mars. We shall be passing there one day, of course, though not I fear for some time. However, time is no longer a consideration to you. I believe you are to spend the entire voyage in sleep. But a very pleasantly coloured sleep nonetheless.' He smiled roguishly at Margot.

As he reached the door Clifford managed to gasp out: 'Where are we? For heaven's sake, call the police!'

Captain Linstrom paused in surprise. 'But surely you know, Mr Gorrell?' He strode to the window and flung back the curtains. In place of the large square casement were three small portholes. Outside a blaze of incandescent light flashed by, a rush of stars and nebulae.

Captain Linstrom gestured theatrically. 'This is the *Dream of Osiris*, under charter to Terminal Tours, three hours out from Zenith City on the non-stop run. May I wish you sweet dreams!'

Escapement

Neither of us was watching the play too closely when I first noticed the slip. I was stretched back in front of the fire with the cross-word, braising gently and toying with 17 down ('told by antique clocks? 5, 5.') while Helen was hemming an old petticoat, looking up only when the third lead, a heavy-chinned youth with a 42-inch neck and a base-surge voice, heaved manfully downscreen. The play was 'My Sons, My Sons,' one of those Thursday night melodramas Channel 2 put out through the winter months, and had been running for about an hour; we'd reached that ebb somewhere round Act 3 Scene 3 just after the old farmer learns that his sons no longer respect him. The whole play must have been recorded on film, and it sounded extremely funny to switch from the old man's broken mutterings back to the showdown sequence fifteen minutes earlier when the eldest son starts drumming his chest and dragging in the high symbols. Somewhere an engineer was out of a job.

'They've got their reels crossed,' I told Helen. 'This is where we came in.'

'Is it?' she said looking up. 'I wasn't watching. Tap the set.'

'Just wait and see. In a moment everyone in the studio will start apologizing.'

Helen peered at the screen. 'I don't think we've seen this,' she said. 'I'm sure we haven't. Quiet.'

I shrugged and went back to 17 down, thinking vaguely about sand dials and water clocks. The scene dragged on; the old man stood his ground, ranted over his turnips and thundered desperately for Ma. The studio must have decided to run it straight through again and pretend no-one had noticed. Even so they'd be fifteen minutes behind their schedule.

Ten minutes later it happened again.

I sat up. 'That's funny,' I said slowly. 'Haven't they spotted it yet? They can't all be asleep.'

'What's the matter?' Helen asked, looking up from her needle basket. 'Is something wrong with the set?'

'I thought you were watching. I told you we'd seen this before. Now they're playing it back for the third time.'

'They're not,' Helen insisted. 'I'm sure they aren't. You must have read the book.'

'Heaven forbid.' I watched the set closely. Any minute now an announcer spitting on a sandwich would splutter red-faced to the screen. I'm not one of those people who reach for their phones every time someone mispronounces meteorology, but this time I knew there'd be thousands who'd feel it their duty to keep the studio exchanges blocked all night. And for any go-ahead comedian on a rival station the lapse was a god-send.

'Do you mind if I change the programme?' I asked Helen. 'See if anything else is on.'

'Don't. This is the most interesting part of the play. You'll spoil it.'

'Darling, you're not even watching. I'll come back to it in a moment, I promise.'

On Channel 5 a panel of three professors and a chorus girl were staring hard at a Roman pot. The question-master, a suave-voiced Oxford don, kept up a lot of crazy patter about scraping the bottom of the barrow. The professors seemed stumped, but the girl looked as if she knew exactly what went into the pot but didn't dare say it.

On 9 there was a lot of studio laughter and someone was giving a sports-car to an enormous woman in a cartwheel hat. The woman nervously ducked her head away from the camera and stared glumly at the car. The compère opened the door for her and I was wondering whether she'd try to get into it when Helen cut in:

'Harry don't be mean. You're just playing.'

I turned back to the play on Channel 2. The same scene was on, nearing the end of its run.

'Now watch it,' I told Helen. She usually managed to catch on the third time round. 'Put that sewing away, it's getting on my nerves. God, I know this off by heart.'

'Sh!' Helen told me. 'Can't you stop talking?'

I lit a cigarette and lay back in the sofa, waiting. The apologies, to say the least, would have to be magniloquent. Two ghost runs at £100 a minute totted up to a tidy heap of doubloons.

The scene drew to a close, the old man stared heavily at his boots, the dusk drew down and –

We were back where we started from.

'Fantastic!' I said, standing up and turning some snow off the screen. 'It's incredible.'

'I didn't know you enjoyed this sort of play,' Helen said calmly. 'You never used to.' She glanced over at the screen and then went back to her petticoat.

I watched her warily. A million years earlier I'd probably have run howling out of the cave and flung myself thankfully under the nearest dinosaur. Nothing in the meanwhile had lessened the dangers hemming in the undaunted husband.

'Darling,' I explained patiently, just keeping the edge out of my voice, 'in case you hadn't noticed they are now playing this same scene through for the fourth time.'

'The fourth time?' Helen said doubtfully. 'Are they repeating it?'

I was visualizing a studio full of announcers and engineers slumped unconscious over their mikes and valves, while an automatic camera pumped out the same reel. Eerie but unlikely. There were monitor receivers as well as the critics, agents, sponsors, and, unforgivably, the playwright himself weighing every minute and every word in their private currencies. They'd all have a lot to say under tomorrow's headlines.

'Sit down and stop fidgeting,' Helen said. 'Have you lost your bone?'

I felt round the cushions and ran my hand along the carpet below the sofa.

'My cigarette,' I said. 'I must have thrown it into the fire. I don't think I dropped it.'

I turned back to the set and switched on the give-away programme, noting the time, 9.03, so that I could get back to Channel 2 at 9.15. When the explanation came I just had to hear it.

'I thought you were enjoying the play,' Helen said. 'Why've you turned it off?'

I gave her what sometimes passes in our flat for a withering frown and settled back.

The enormous woman was still at it in front of the cameras, working her way up a pyramid of questions on cookery. The audience was subdued but interest mounted. Eventually she answered the jackpot question and the audience roared and thumped their seats like a lot of madmen. The compère led her across the stage to another sports car.

61

'She'll have a stable of them soon,' I said aside to Helen.

The woman shook hands and awkwardly dipped the brim of her hat, smiling nervously with embarrassment.

The gesture was oddly familiar.

I jumped up and switched to Channel 5. The panel were still staring hard at their pot.

Then I started to realize what was going on.

All three programmes were repeating themselves.

'Helen,' I said over my shoulder. 'Get me a scotch and soda, will you?'

'What *is* the matter? Have you strained your back?'

'Quickly, quickly!' I snapped my fingers.

'Hold on.' She got up and went into the pantry.

I looked at the time. 9.12. Then I returned to the play and kept my eyes glued to the screen. Helen came back and put something down on the end-table.

'There you are. You all right?'

When it switched I thought I was ready for it, but the surprise must have knocked me flat. I found myself lying out on the sofa. The first thing I did was reach round for the drink.

'Where did you put it?' I asked Helen.

'What?'

'The Scotch. You brought it in a couple of minutes ago. It was on the table.'

'You've been dreaming,' she said gently. She leant forward and started watching the play.

I went into the pantry and found the bottle. As I filled a tumbler I noticed the clock over the kitchen sink. 9.07. An hour slow, now that I thought about it. But my wrist-watch said 9.05, and always ran perfectly. And the clock on the mantlepiece in the lounge also said 9.05.

Before I really started worrying I had to make sure.

Mullvaney, our neighbour in the flat above, opened his door when I knocked.

'Hello, Bartley. Corkscrew?'

'No, no,' I told him. 'What's the right time? Our clocks are going crazy.'

He glanced at his wrist. 'Nearly ten past.'

'Nine or ten?'

He looked at his watch again. 'Nine, should be. What's up?'

'I don't know whether I'm losing my – ' I started to say. Then I stopped.

Mullvaney eyed me curiously. Over his shoulder I heard a wave of studio applause, broken by the creamy, unctuous voice of the give-away compère.

'How long's that programme been on?' I asked him.

'About twenty minutes. Aren't you watching?'

'No,' I said, adding casually. 'Is anything wrong with your set?'

He shook his head. 'Nothing. Why?'

'Mine's chasing its tail. Anyway, thanks.'

'OK,' he said. He watched me go down the stairs and shrugged as he shut his door.

I went into the hall, picked up the phone and dialled.

'Hello, Tom?' Tom Farnold works the desk next to mine at the office. 'Tom, Harry here. What time do you make it?'

'Time the liberals were back.'

'No, seriously.'

'Let's see. Twelve past nine. By the way, did you find those pickles I left for you in the safe?'

'Yeah, thanks. Listen, Tom,' I went on, 'the goddamdest things are happening here. We were watching Diller's play on Channel 2 when – '

'I'm watching it now. Hurry it up.'

'You are? Well, how do you explain this repetition business? And the way the clocks are stuck between 9 and 9.15?'

Tom laughed. 'I don't know,' he said. 'I suggest you go outside and give the house a shake.'

I reached out for the glass I had with me on the hall table, wondering how to explain to –

The next moment I found myself back on the sofa. I was holding the newspaper and looking at 17 down. A part of my mind was thinking about antique clocks.

I pulled myself out of it and glanced across at Helen. She was sitting quietly with her needle basket. The all too familiar play was repeating itself and by the clock on the mantelpiece it was still just after 9.

I went back into the hall and dialled Tom again, trying not to stampede myself. In some way, I hadn't begun to understand how, a section of time was spinning round in a circle, with myself in the centre.

'Tom,' I asked quickly as soon as he picked up the phone. 'Did I call you five minutes ago?'

'Who's that again?'

'Harry here. Harry Bartley. Sorry Tom.' I paused and rephrased the question, trying to make it sound intelligible. 'Tom, did you phone me up about five minutes ago? We've had a little trouble with the line here.'

'No,' he told me. 'Wasn't me. By the way, did you get those pickles I left in the safe?'

'Thanks a lot,' I said, beginning to panic. 'Are you watching the play, Tom?'

'Yes. I think I'll get back to it. See you.'

I went into the kitchen and had a long close look at myself in the mirror. A crack across it dropped one side of my face three inches below the other, but apart from that I couldn't see anything that added up to a psychosis. My eyes seemed steady, pulse was in the low seventies, no tics or clammy traumatic sweat. Everything around me seemed much too solid and authentic for a dream.

I waited for a minute and then went back to the lounge and sat down. Helen was watching the play.

I leant forward and turned the knob round. The picture dimmed and swayed off.

'Harry, I'm watching that! Don't switch if off.'

I went over to her. 'Poppet,' I said, holding my voice together. 'Listen to me, please. Very carefully. It's important.'

She frowned, put her sewing down and took my hands.

'For some reason, I don't know why, we seem to be in a sort of circular time trap, just going round and round. You're not aware of it, and I can't find anyone else who is either.'

Helen stared at me in amazement. 'Harry,' she started, 'what are you – '

'Helen!' I insisted, gripping her shoulders. 'Listen! For the last two hours a section of time about 15 minutes long has been repeating itself. The clocks are stuck between 9 and 9.15. That play you're watching has – '

'Harry, darling.' She looked at me and smiled helplessly. 'You are silly. Now turn it on again.'

I gave up.

As I switched the set on I ran through all the other channels just to see if anything had changed.

The panel stared at their pot, the fat woman won her sports car, the old farmer ranted. On Channel 1, the old BBC service which put out a couple of hours on alternate evenings, two newspaper men were interviewing a scientific pundit who appeared on popular educational programmes.

'What effect these dense eruptions of gas will have so far it's impossible to tell. However, there's certainly no cause for any alarm. These billows have mass, and I think we can expect a lot of strange optical effects as the light leaving the sun is deflected by them gravitationally.'

He started playing with a set of coloured celluloid balls running on concentric metal rings, and fiddled with a ripple tank mounted against a mirror on the table.

One of the newsmen asked: 'What about the relationship between light and time? If I remember my relativity they're tied up together pretty closely. Are you sure we won't all need to add another hand to our clocks and watches?'

The pundit smiled. 'I think we'll be able to get along without that. Time is extremely complicated, but I can assure you the clocks won't suddenly start running backwards or sideways.'

I listened to him until Helen began to remonstrate. I switched the play on for her and went off into the hall. The fool didn't know what he was talking about. What I couldn't understand was why I was the only person who realized what was going on. If I could get Tom over I might just be able to convince him.

I picked up the phone and glanced at my watch.

9.13. By the time I got through to Tom the next changeover would be due. Somehow I didn't like the idea of being picked up and flung to the sofa, however painless it might be. I put the phone down and went into the lounge.

The jump-back was smoother than I expected. I wasn't conscious of anything, not even the slightest tremor. A phrase was stuck in my mind: Olden Times.

The newspaper was back on my lap, folded around the crossword. I looked through the clues.

17 down: Told by antique clocks? 5, 5.

I must have solved it sub-consciously.

I remembered that I'd intended to phone Tom.

'Hullo, Tom?' I asked when I got through. 'Harry here.'

'Did you get those pickles I left in the safe?'

'Yes, thanks a lot. Tom, could you come round tonight? Sorry to ask you this late, but it's fairly urgent.'

'Yes, of course,' he said. 'What's the trouble?'

'I'll tell you when you get here. As soon as you can?'

'Sure. I'll leave right away. Is Helen all right?'

'Yes, she's fine. Thanks again.'

I went into the dining-room and pulled a bottle of gin and a couple of tonics out of the sideboard. He'd need a drink when he heard what I had to say.

Then I realized he'd never make it. From Earls Court it would take him at least half an hour to reach us at Maida Vale and he'd probably get no further than Marble Arch.

I filled my glass out of the virtually bottomless bottle of Scotch and tried to work out a plan of action.

The first step was to get hold of someone like myself who retained his awareness of the past switch-backs. Somewhere else there must be others trapped in their little 15-minute cages who were also wondering desperately how to get out. I could start by phoning everyone I knew and then going on at random through the phone-book. But what could we do if we did find each other? In fact there was nothing to do except sit tight and wait for it all to wear off. At least I knew I wasn't looping my loop. Once these billows or whatever they were had burnt themselves out we'd be able to get off the round-about.

Until then I had an unlimited supply of whisky waiting for me in the half-empty bottle standing on the sink, though of course there was one snag: I'd never be able to get drunk.

I was musing round some of the other possibilities available and wondering how to get a permanent record of what was going on when an idea hit me.

I got out the phone-directory and looked up the number of KBC-TV, Channel 9.

A girl at reception answered the phone. After haggling with her for a couple of minutes I persuaded her to put me through to one of the producers.

'Hullo,' I said. 'Is the jack-pot question in tonight's programme known to any members of the studio audience?'

'No, of course not.'

'I see. As a matter of interest, do you yourself know it?'

'No,' he said. 'All the questions tonight are known only to our senior programme producer and M. Phillipe Soisson of Savoy Hotels Limited. They're a closely guarded secret.'

'Thanks,' I said. 'If you've got a piece of paper handy I'll give you the jack-pot question. "List the complete menu at the Guildhall Coronation Banquet in July 1953."'

There were muttered consultations, and a second voice came through.

'Who's that speaking?'

'Mr H.R. Bartley, 129b Sutton Court Road, N.W. – '

Before I could finish I found myself back in the lounge.

The jump-back had caught me. But instead of being stretched out on the sofa I was standing up, leaning on one elbow against the mantelpiece, looking down at the newspaper.

My eyes were focused clearly on the cross-word puzzle, and before I pulled them away and started thinking over my call to the studio I noticed something that nearly dropped me into the grate.

17 down had been filled in.

I picked up the paper and showed it to Helen.

'Did you do this clue? 17 down?'

'No,' she said. 'I never even look at the cross-word.'

The clock on the mantelpiece caught my eye, and I forgot about the studio and playing tricks with other people's time.

9.03.

The merry-go-round was closing in. I thought the jump-back had come sooner than I expected. At least two minutes earlier, somewhere around 9.13.

And not only was the repetition interval getting shorter, but as the arc edged inwards on itself it was uncovering the real time stream running below it, the stream in which the other I, unknown to myself here, had solved the clue, stood up, walked over to the mantelpiece and filled in 17 down.

I sat down on the sofa, watching the clock carefully.

★ ★ ★

For the first time that evening Helen was thumbing over the pages of a magazine. The work-basket was tucked away on the bottom shelf of the bookcase.

'Do you want this on any longer?' she asked me. 'It's not very good.'

I turned to the panel game. The three professors and the chorus girl were still playing around with their pot.

On Channel 1 the pundit was sitting at the table with his models.

'. . . alarm. The billows have mass, and I think we can expect a lot of strange optical effects as the light – '

I switched it off.

The next jump-back came at 9.11. Somewhere I'd left the mantelpiece, gone back to the sofa and lit a cigarette.

It was 9.04. Helen had opened the verandah windows and was looking out into the street.

The set was on again so I pulled the plug out at the main. I threw the cigarette into the fire; not having seen myself light it, made it taste like someone else's.

'Harry, like to go out for a stroll?' Helen suggested. 'It'll be rather nice in the park.'

Each successive jump-back gave us a new departure point. If now I bundled her outside and got her down to the end of the road, at the next jump we'd both be back in the lounge again, but probably have decided to drive to the pub instead.

'Harry?'

'What, sorry?'

'Are you asleep, angel? Like to go for a walk? It'll wake you up.'

'All right,' I said. 'Go and get your coat.'

'Will you be warm enough like that?'

She went off into the bedroom

I walked round the lounge and convinced myself that I was awake. The shadows, the solid feel of the chairs, the definition was much too fine for a dream.

It was 9.08. Normally Helen would take ten minutes to put on her coat.

The jump-back came almost immediately.

It was 9.06.

I was still on the sofa and Helen was bending down and picking up her work basket.

This time, at last, the set was off.

'Have you got any money on you?' Helen asked.

I felt in my pocket automatically. 'Yes. How much do you want?'

Helen looked at me. 'Well, what do you usually pay for the drinks? We'll only have a couple.'

'We're going to the pub, are we?'

'Darling, are you all right?' She came over to me. 'You look all strangled. Is that shirt too tight?'

'Helen,' I said, getting up. 'I've got to try to explain something to you. I don't know why it's happening, it's something to do with these billows of gas the sun's releasing.'

Helen was watching me with her mouth open.

'Harry,' she started to say nervously. 'What's the matter?'

'I'm quite all right,' I assured her. 'It's just that everything is happening very rapidly and I don't think there's much time left.'

I kept on glancing at the clock and Helen followed my eyes to it and went over to the mantelpiece. Watching me she moved it round and I heard the pendulum jangle.

'No, no,' I shouted. I grabbed it and pushed it back against the wall.

We jumped back to 9.07.

Helen was in the bedroom. I had exactly a minute left.

'Harry,' she called. 'Darling, do you want to, or don't you?'

I was by the lounge window, muttering something.

I was out of touch with what my real self was doing in the normal time channel. The Helen talking to me now was a phantom.

It was I, not Helen and everybody else, who was riding the merry-go-round.

Jump.

9.07-15.

Helen was standing in the doorway.

'. . . down to the . . . the . . . ' I was saying.

Helen watched me, frozen. A fraction of a minute left.

I started to walk over to her.

to walk over to her

ver to her

er

I came out of it like a man catapulted from a revolving door. I was stretched out flat on the sofa, a hard aching pain running from the top of my head down past my right ear into my neck.

I looked at the time. 9.45. I could hear Helen moving around in the dining-room. I lay there, steadying the room round me, and in a few minutes she came in carrying a tray and a couple of glasses.

'How do you feel?' she asked, making up an alka-seltzer.

I let it fizzle down and drank it.

'What happened?' I asked. 'Did I collapse?'

'Not exactly. You were watching the play. I thought you looked rather seedy so I suggested we go out for a drink. You went into a sort of convulsion.'

I stood up slowly and rubbed my neck. 'God, I didn't dream all that! I couldn't have done.'

'What was it about?'

'A sort of crazy merry-go-round – ' The pain grabbed at my neck when I spoke. I went over to the set and switched it on. 'Hard to explain coherently. Time was – ' I flinched as the pain bit in again.

'Sit down and rest,' Helen said. 'I'll come and join you. Like a drink?'

'Thanks. A big Scotch.'

I looked at the set. On Channel 1 there was a breakdown sign, a cabaret on 2, a flood-lit stadium on 5, and a variety show on 9. No sign anywhere of either Diller's play or the panel game.

Helen brought the drink in and sat down on the sofa with me.

'It started off when we were watching the play,' I explained, massaging my neck.

'Sh, don't bother now. Just relax.'

I put my head on Helen's shoulder and looked up at the ceiling, listening to the sound coming from the variety show. I thought back through each turn of the round-about, wondering whether I could have dreamt it all.

Ten minutes later Helen said, 'Well, I didn't think much of that. And they're doing an encore. Good heavens.'

'Who are?' I asked. I watched the light from the screen flicker across her face.

'That team of acrobats. The something Brothers. One of them even slipped. How do you feel?'

'Fine.' I turned my head round and looked at the screen.

Three or four acrobats with huge v-torsos and skin briefs were doing simple handstands on to each other's arms. They finished the act and went into a more involved routine, throwing around a girl in leopard skin panties. The applause was deafening. I thought they were moderately good.

Two of them began to give what seemed to be a demonstration of dynamic tension, straining against each other like a pair of catatonic bulls, their necks and legs locked, until one of them was levered slowly off the ground.

'Why do they keep on doing that?' Helen said. 'They've done it twice already.'

'I don't think they have,' I said. 'This is a slightly different act.'

The pivot man tremored, one of his huge banks of muscles collapsed, and the whole act toppled and then sprung apart.

'They slipped there the last time,' Helen said.

'No, no,' I pointed out quickly. 'That one was a headstand. Here they were stretched out horizontally.'

'You weren't watching,' Helen told me. She leant forward. 'Well, what are they playing at? They're repeating the whole thing for the third time.'

It was an entirely new act to me, but I didn't try to argue.

I sat up and looked at the clock.

10.05.

'Darling,' I said, putting my arm round her. 'Hold tight.'

'What do you mean?'

'This is the merry-go-round. And you're driving.'

Time of Passage

Sunlight spilled among the flowers and tombstones, turning the cemetery into a bright garden of sculpture. Like two large gaunt crows, the gravediggers leaned on their spades between the marble angels, their shadows arching across the smooth white flank of one of the recent graves.

The gilt lettering was still fresh and untarnished.

JAMES FALKMAN
1963–1901
'The End is but the Beginning'

Leisurely they began to pare back the crisp turf, then dismantled the headstone and swathed it in a canvas sheet, laying it behind the graves in the next aisle. Biddle, the older of the two, a lean man in a black waistcoat, pointed to the cemetery gates, where the first mourning party approached.

'They're here. Let's get our backs into it.'

The younger man, Biddle's son, watched the small procession winding through the graves. His nostrils scented the sweet broken earth. 'They're always early,' he murmured reflectively. 'It's a strange thing, you never see them come on time.'

A clock tolled from the chapel among the cypresses. Working swiftly, they scooped out the soft earth, piling it into a neat cone at the grave's head. A few minutes later, when the sexton arrived with the principal mourners, the polished teak of the coffin was exposed, and Biddle jumped down on to the lid and scraped away the damp earth clinging to its brass rim.

The ceremony was brief and the twenty mourners, led by Falkman's sister, a tall white-haired woman with a narrow autocratic face, leaning on her husband's arm, soon returned to the chapel. Biddle gestured to his son. They jerked the coffin out of the ground and loaded it on to a cart, strapping it down under the harness. Then they heaped the earth back into the grave and relaid the squares of turf.

As they pushed the cart back to the chapel the sunlight shone brightly among the thinning graves.

Forty-eight hours later the coffin arrived at James Falkman's large grey-stoned house on the upper slopes of Mortmere Park. The high-walled avenue was almost deserted and few people saw the hearse enter the tree-lined drive. The blinds were drawn over the windows, and huge wreaths rested among the furniture in the hall where Falkman lay motionless in his coffin on a mahogany table. Veiled by the dim light, his square strong-jawed face seemed composed and unblemished, a short lock of hair over his forehead making his expression less severe than his sister's.

A solitary beam of sunlight, finding its way through the dark sycamores which guarded the house, slowly traversed the room as the morning progressed, and shone for a few minutes upon Falkman's open eyes. Even after the beam had moved away a faint glimmer of light still remained in the pupils, like the reflection of a star glimpsed in the bottom of a dark well.

All day, helped by two of her friends, sharp-faced women in long black coats, Falkman's sister moved quietly about the house. Her quick deft hands shook the dust from the velvet curtains in the library, wound up the miniature Louis XV clock on the study desk, and reset the great barometer on the staircase. None of the women spoke to each other, but within a few hours the house was transformed, the dark wood in the hall gleaming as the first callers were admitted.

'Mr and Mrs Montefiore . . . '

'Mr and Mrs Caldwell . . . '

'Miss Evelyn Jermyn and Miss Elizabeth . . . '

'Mr Samuel Banbury . . . '

One by one nodding in acknowledgement as they were announced, the callers trooped into the hall and paused over the coffin, examining Falkman's face with discreet interest, then passed into the dining-room where they were presented with a glass of port and a tray of sweet-meats. Most of them were elderly, over-dressed in the warm spring weather, one or two obviously ill at ease in the great oak-panelled house, and all unmistakably revealed the same air of hushed expectancy.

The following morning Falkman was lifted from his coffin and carried upstairs to the bedroom overlooking the drive. The winding sheet was removed from his frail body dressed in a pair of thick woollen pyjamas. He lay quietly between the cold sheets, his grey face sightless and reposed, unaware of his sister crying softly on the high-backed chair beside him. Only when Dr Markham called and put his hand on her shoulder did she contain herself, relieved to have given way to her feelings.

Almost as if this were a signal, Falkman opened his eyes. For a moment they wavered uncertainly, the pupils weak and watery. Then he gazed up at his sister's tear-marked face, his head motionless on the pillow. As she and the doctor leaned forward Falkman smiled fleetingly, his lips parting across his teeth in an expression of immense patience and understanding. Then apparently exhausted he lapsed into a deep sleep.

After securing the blinds over the windows, his sister and the doctor stepped from the room. Below, the doors closed quietly into the drive, and the house became silent. Gradually the sounds of Falkman's breathing grew more steady and filled the bedroom, overlayed by the swaying of the dark trees outside.

So James Falkman made his arrival. For the next week he lay quietly in his bedroom, his strength increasing hourly, and managed to eat his first meals prepared by his sister. She sat in the blackwood chair, her mourning habit exchanged for a grey woollen dress, examining him critically.

'Now James, you'll have to get a better appetite than that. Your poor body is completely wasted.'

Falkman pushed away the tray and let his long slim hands fall across his chest. He smiled amiably at his sister. 'Careful, Betty, or you'll turn me into a milk pudding.'

His sister briskly straightened the eiderdown. 'If you don't like my cooking, James, you can fend for yourself.'

A faint chuckle slipped between Falkman's lips. 'Thank you for telling me, Betty, I fully intend to.'

He lay back, smiling weakly to himself as his sister stalked out with the tray. Teasing her did him almost as much good as the meals she prepared, and he felt the blood reaching down into his cold feet. His face was still grey and flaccid, and he conserved his strength carefully, only his eyes moving as he watched the ravens alighting on the window ledge.

Gradually, as his conversations with his sister became more

frequent, Falkman gained sufficient strength to sit up. He began to take a fuller interest in the world around him, watching the people in the avenue through the french windows and disputing his sister's commentary on them.

'There's Sam Banbury again,' she remarked testily as a small leprechaunlike old man hobbled past. 'Off to the Swan as usual. When's he going to get a job, I'd like to know.'

'Be more charitable, Betty. Sam's a very sensible fellow. I'd rather go to the pub than have a job.'

His sister snorted sceptically, her assessment of Falkman's character apparently at variance with this statement. 'You've got one of the finest houses in Mortmere Park,' she told him. 'I think you should be more careful with people like Sam Banbury. He's not in your class, James.'

Falkman smiled patiently at his sister. 'We're all in the same class, or have you been here so long you've forgotten, Betty.'

'We all forget,' she told him soberly. 'You will too, James. It's sad, but we're in this world now, and we must concern ourselves with it. If the church can keep the memory alive for us, so much the better. As you'll find out though, the majority of folk remember nothing. Perhaps it's a good thing.'

She grudgingly admitted the first visitors, fussing about so that Falkman could barely exchange a word with them. In fact, the visits tired him, and he could do little more than pass a few formal pleasantries. Even when Sam Banbury brought him a pipe and tobacco pouch he had to muster all his energy to thank him and had none left to prevent his sister from making off with them.

Only when the Reverend Matthews called did Falkman manage to summon together his strength, for half an hour spoke earnestly to the parson, who listened with rapt attention, interjecting a few eager questions. When the Reverend left he seemed refreshed and confident, and strode down the stairs with a gay smile at Falkman's sister.

Within three weeks Falkman was out of bed, and managed to hobble downstairs and inspect the house and garden. His sister protested, dogging his slow painful footsteps with sharp reminders of his feebleness, but Falkman ignored her. He found his way to the conservatory, and leaned against one of the ornamental columns, his nervous fingers feeling the leaves of the miniature trees, the scent of flowers flushing his face. Outside, in the grounds, he examined everything around him, as if comparing it with some Elysian paradise in his mind.

He was walking back to the house when he twisted his ankle sharply in the crazy paving. Before he could cry for help he had fallen headlong across the hard stone.

'James Falkman will you never listen?' his sister protested, as she helped him across the terrace. 'I warned you to stay in bed!'

Reaching the lounge, Falkman sat down thankfully in an armchair, reassembling his stunned limbs. 'Quiet, Betty, do you mind,' he admonished his sister when his breath returned. 'I'm still here, and I'm perfectly well.'

He had stated no more than the truth. After the accident he began to recover spectacularly, his progress toward complete health accelerating without a break, as if the tumble had freed him from the lingering fatigue and discomfort of the previous weeks. His step became brisk and lively, his complexion brightened, a soft pink glow filling out his cheeks, and he moved busily around the house.

A month afterwards his sister returned to her own home, acknowledging his ability to look after himself, and her place was taken by the housekeeper. After re-establishing himself in the house, Falkman became increasingly interested in the world outside. He hired a comfortable car and chauffeur, and spent most of the winter afternoons and evenings at his club; soon he found himself the centre of a wide circle of acquaintances. He became the chairman of a number of charitable committees, where his good humour, tolerance and shrewd judgement made him well respected. He now held himself erect, his grey hair sprouting luxuriantly, here and there touched by black flecks, jaw jutting firmly from sun-tanned cheeks.

Every Sunday he attended the morning and evening services at his church, where he owned a private pew, and was somewhat saddened to see that only the older people formed the congregation. However, he himself found that the picture painted by the liturgy became increasingly detached from his own memories as the latter faded, too soon became a meaningless charade that he could accept only by an act of faith.

A few years later, when he became increasingly restless, he decided to accept the offer of a partnership in a leading firm of stockbrokers.

★　★　★

Many of his acquaintances at the club were also finding jobs, forsaking the placid routines of smoking room and conservatory garden. Harold Caldwell, one of his closest friends, was appointed Professor of History at the university, and Sam Banbury became manager of the Swan Hotel.

The ceremony on Falkman's first day at the stock exchange was dignified and impressive. Three junior men also joining the firm were introduced to the assembled staff by the senior partner, Mr Montefiore, and each presented with a gold watch to symbolize the years he would spend with the firm. Falkman received an embossed silver cigar case and was loudly applauded.

For the next five years Falkman threw himself wholeheartedly into his work, growing more extrovert and aggressive as his appetite for the material pleasures of life increased. He became a keen golfer; then, as the exercise strengthened his physique, played his first games of tennis. An influential member of the business community, his days passed in a pleasant round of conferences and dinner parties. He no longer attended the church, but instead spent his Sundays escorting the more attractive of his lady acquaintances to the race tracks and regattas.

He found it all the more surprising, therefore when a persistent mood of dejection began to haunt him. Although without any apparent source, this deepened slowly, and he found himself reluctant to leave his house in the evenings. He resigned from his committees and no longer visited his club. At the stock exchange he felt permanently distracted, and would stand for hours by the window, staring down at the traffic.

Finally, when his grasp of the business began to slip, Mr Montefiore suggested that he go on indefinite leave.

For a week Falkman listlessly paced around the huge empty house. Sam Banbury frequently called to see him, but Falkman's sense of grief was beyond any help. He drew the blinds over the windows and changed into a black tie and suit, sat blankly in the darkened library.

At last, when his depression had reached its lowest ebb, he went to the cemetery to collect his wife.

After the congregation had dispersed, Falkman paused outside the vestry to tip the gravedigger, Biddle, and compliment him on his young son, a cherubic three-year old who was playing among the headstones. Then he rode back to Mortmere Park in the car following the hearse, the remainder of the cortege behind him.

'A grand turnout, James,' his sister told him approvingly. 'Twenty cars altogether, not including the private ones.'

Falkman thanked her, his eyes examining his sister with critical detachment. In the fifteen years he had known her she had coarsened perceptibly, her voice roughening and her gestures becoming broader. A distinct social gap had always separated them, a division which Falkman had accepted charitably, but it was now widening markedly. Her husband's business had recently begun to fail, and her thoughts had turned almost exclusively to the subjects of money and social prestige.

As Falkman congratulated himself on his good sense and success, a curious premonition, indistinct but nonetheless disturbing, stirred through his mind.

Like Falkman himself fifteen years earlier, his wife first lay in her coffin in the hall, the heavy wreaths transforming it into a dark olive-green bower. Behind the lowered blinds the air was dim and stifled, and with her rich red hair flaring off her forehead, and her broad cheeks and full lips, his wife seemed to Falkman like some sleeping enchantress in a magical arbor. He gripped the silver foot rail of the coffin and stared at her mindlessly, aware of his sister shepherding the guests to the port and whisky. He traced with his eyes the exquisite dips and hollows around his wife's neck and chin, the white skin sweeping smoothly to her strong shoulders. The next day, when she was carried upstairs, her presence filled the bedroom. All afternoon he sat beside her, waiting patiently for her to wake.

Shortly after five o'clock, in the few minutes of light left before the dusk descended, when the air hung motionlessly under the trees in the garden, a faint echo of life moved across her face. Her eyes cleared and then focused on the ceiling.

Breathlessly, Falkman leaned forward and took one of her cold hands. Far within, the pulse sounded faintly.

'Marion,' he whispered.

Her head inclined slightly, lips parting in a weak smile. For several moments she gazed serenely at her husband.

'Hello, Jamie.'

His wife's arrival completely rejuvenated Falkman. A devoted husband, he was soon completely immersed in their life together. As she recovered from the long illness after her arrival, Falkman entered the prime of his life. His grey hair became sleek and black, his face grew thicker, the chin firmer and stronger. He returned to the stock exchange, taking up his job with renewed interest.

He and Marion made a handsome couple. At intervals they would visit the cemetery and join in the service celebrating the arrival of another of their friends, but these became less frequent. Other parties continually visited the cemetery, thinning the ranks of graves, and large areas had reverted to open lawn as the coffins were withdrawn and the tombstones removed. The firm of undertakers near the cemetery which was responsible for notifying mourning relatives closed down and was sold. Finally, after the gravedigger, Biddle, recovered his own wife from the last of the graves the cemetery was converted into a children's playground.

The years of their marriage were Falkman's happiest. With each successive summer Marion became slimmer and more youthful, her red hair a brilliant diadem that stood out among the crowds in the street when she came to see him. They would walk home arm in arm, in the summer evening pause among the willows by the river to embrace each other like lovers.

Indeed, their happiness became such a byword among their friends that over two hundred guests attended the church ceremony celebrating the long years of their marriage. As they knelt together at the altar before the priest Marion seemed to Falkman like a demure rose.

This was the last night they were to spend together. Over the years Falkman had become less interested in his work at the stock exchange, and the arrival of older and more serious men had resulted in a series of demotions for him. Many of his friends were facing similar problems. Harold Caldwell had been forced to resign his professorship and was now a junior lecturer, taking post-graduate courses to familiarize himself with the great body of new work that had been done in the previous thirty years. Sam Banbury was a waiter at the Swan Hotel.

Marion went to live with her parents, and the Falkmans' apartment, to which they had moved some years earlier after the house was closed and sold, was let to new tenants. Falkman, whose tastes had become simpler as the years passed, took a room in a hostel for young men, but he and Marion saw each other every evening. He felt increasingly restless, half conscious that his life was moving towards an inescapable focus, and often thought of giving up his job.

Marion remonstrated with him. 'But you'll lose everything you've worked for, Jamie. All those years.'

Falkman shrugged, chewing on a stem of grass as they lay in the park during one of their lunch hours. Marion was now a salesgirl in a department store.

'Perhaps, but I resent being demoted. Even Montefiore is leaving. His grandfather has just been appointed chairman.' He rolled over and put his head in her lap. 'It's so dull in that stuffy office, with all those pious old men. I'm not satisfied with it any longer.'

Marion smiled affectionately at his naïvete and enthusiasm. Falkman was now more handsome than she had ever remembered him, his sun-tanned face almost unlined.

'It's been wonderful together, Marion,' he told her on the eve of their thirtieth anniversary. 'How lucky we've been never to have a child. Do you realize that some people even have three or four? It's absolutely tragic.'

'It comes to us all, though, Jamie,' she reminded him. 'Some people say it's a very beautiful and noble experience, having a child.'

All evening he and Marion wandered round the town together, Falkman's desire for her quickened by her increasing demureness. Since she had gone to live with her parents Marion had become almost too shy to take his hand.

Then he lost her.

Walking through the market in the town centre, they were joined by two of Marion's friends, Elizabeth and Evelyn Jermyn.

'There's Sam Banbury,' Evelyn pointed out as a firework crackled from a stall on the other side of the market. 'Playing the fool as usual.' She and her sister clucked disapprovingly. Tight-mouthed and stern, they wore dark serge coats buttoned to their necks.

Distracted by Sam, Falkman wandered off a few steps, suddenly found that the three girls had walked away. Darting through the crowd, he tried to catch up with them, briefly glimpsed Marion's red hair.

He fought his way through the stalls, almost knocking over a barrow of vegetables and shouted at Sam Banbury:

'Sam! Have you seen Marion?'

Banbury pocketed his crackers and helped him to scan the crowd. For an hour they searched. Finally Sam gave up and went home, leaving Falkman to hang about the cobbled square under the dim lights when the market closed, wandering among the tinsel and litter as the stall holders packed up for home.

'Excuse me, have you seen a girl here? A girl with red hair?'

'Please, she was here this afternoon.'

'A girl . . . '

' . . . called . . . '

Stunned, he realized that he had forgotten her name.

Shortly afterwards, Falkman gave up his job and went to live with his parents. Their small red-brick house was on the opposite side of the town; between the crowded chimney pots he could sometimes see the distant slopes of Mortmere Park. His life now began a less carefree phase, as most of his energy went into helping his mother and looking after his sister Betty. By comparison with his own house his parents' home was bleak and uncomfortable, altogether alien to everything Falkman had previously known. Although kind and respectable people, his parents' lives were circumscribed by their lack of success or education. They had no interest in music or the theatre, and Falkman found his mind beginning to dull and coarsen.

His father was openly critical of him for leaving his job, but the hostility between them gradually subsided as he more and more began to dominate Falkman, restricting his freedom and reducing his pocket money, even warning him not to play with certain of his friends. In fact, going to live with his parents had taken Falkman into an entirely new world.

By the time he began to go to school Falkman had completely forgotten his past life, his memories of Marion and the great house where they had lived surrounded by servants altogether obliterated.

During his first term at school he was in a class with the older boys, whom the teachers treated as equals, but like his parents they began to extend their influence over him as the years passed. At times Falkman rebelled against this attempt to suppress his own personality, but at last they entirely dominated him, controlling his activities and moulding his thoughts and speech. The whole process of education, he dimly realized, was designed to prepare him for the strange twilight world of his earliest childhood. It deliberately eliminated every trace of sophistication, breaking down, with its constant repetitions and brain-splitting exercises, all his knowledge of language and mathematics, substituting for them a collection of meaningless rhymes, and chants, and out of this constructing an artificial world of total infantilism.

At last, when the process of education had reduced him almost to the stage of an inarticulate infant, his parents intervened by removing him from the school, and the final years of his life were spent at home.

'Mama, can I sleep with you?'

Mrs Falkman looked down at the serious-faced little boy who leaned his head on her pillow. Affectionately she pinched his square jaw and then touched her husband's shoulder as he stirred. Despite the years between father and son, their two bodies were almost identical, with the same broad shoulders and broad heads, the same thick hair.

'Not today, Jamie, but soon perhaps, one day.'

The child watched his mother with wide eyes, wondering why she should be crying to herself, guessing that perhaps he had touched upon one of the taboos that had exercised such a potent fascination for all the boys at school, the mystery of their ultimate destination that remained carefully shrouded by their parents and which they themselves were no longer able to grasp.

By now he was beginning to experience the first difficulties in both walking and feeding himself. He tottered about clumsily, his small piping voice tripping over his tongue. Steadily his vocabulary diminished until he knew only his mother's name. When he could no longer stand upright she would carry him in her arms, feeding him like an elderly invalid. His mind clouded, a few constants of warmth and hunger drifting through it hazily. As long as he could, he clung to his mother.

Shortly afterward, Falkman and his mother visited the lying-in hospital for several weeks. On her return Mrs. Falkman remained in bed for a few days, but gradually she began to move about more freely, slowly shedding the additional weight accumulated during her confinement.

Some nine months after she returned from the hospital, a period during which she and her husband thought continually of their son, the tragedy of his approaching death, a symbol of their own imminent separation, bringing them closer together, they went away on their honeymoon.

The Venus Hunters

When Dr Andrew Ward joined the Hubble Memorial Institute at Mount Vernon Observatory he never imagined that the closest of his new acquaintances would be an amateur star-gazer and spare-time prophet called Charles Kandinski, tolerantly regarded by the Observatory professionals as a madman. In fact, had either he or Professor Cameron, the Institute's Deputy Director, known just how far he was to be prepared to carry this friendship before his two-year tour at the Institute was over, Ward would certainly have left Mount Vernon the day he arrived and would never have become involved in the bizarre and curiously ironic tragedy which was to leave an ineradicable stigma upon his career.

Professor Cameron first introduced him to Kandinski. About a week after Ward came to the Hubble he and Cameron were lunching together in the Institute cafeteria.

'We'll go down to Vernon Gardens for coffee,' Cameron said when they finished dessert. 'I want to get a shampoo for Edna's roses and then we'll sit in the sun for an hour and watch the girls go by.' They strolled out through the terrace tables towards the parking lot. A mile away, beyond the conifers thinning out on the slopes above them, the three great Vernon domes gleamed like white marble against the sky. 'Incidentally, you can meet the opposition.'

'Is there another observatory at Vernon?' Ward asked as they set off along the drive in Cameron's Buick. 'What is it – an Air Force weather station?'

'Have you ever heard of Charles Kandinski?' Cameron said. 'He wrote a book called "The Landings from Outer Space." It was published about three years ago.'

Ward shook his head doubtfully. They slowed down past the check-point at the gates and Cameron waved to the guard. 'Is that the man who claims to have seen extra-terrestrial beings? Martians or – '

'Venusians. That's Kandinski. Not only seen them,' Professor Cameron added. 'He's talked to them. Charles works at a cafe in Vernon Gardens. We know him fairly well.'

'He runs the other observatory?'

'Well, an old 4-inch MacDonald Refractor mounted in a bucket of cement. You probably wouldn't think much of it, but I wish we could see with our two-fifty just a tenth of what he sees.'

Ward nodded vaguely. The two observatories at which he had worked previously, Cape Town and the Milan Astrographie, had both attracted any number of cranks and charlatans eager to reveal their own final truths about the cosmos, and the prospect of meeting Kandinski interested him only slightly. 'What is he?' he asked. 'A practical joker, or just a lunatic?'

Professor Cameron propped his glasses on to his forehead and negotiated a tight hairpin. 'Neither,' he said.

Ward smiled at Cameron, idly studying his plump cherubic face with its puckish mouth and keen eyes. He knew that Cameron enjoyed a modest reputation as a wit. 'Has he ever claimed in front of you that he's seen a . . . Venusian?'

'Often,' Professor Cameron said. 'Charles lectures two or three times a week about the landings to the women's societies around here and put himself completely at our disposal. I'm afraid we had to tell him he was a little too advanced for us. But wait until you meet him.'

Ward shrugged and looked out at the long curving peach terraces lying below them, gold and heavy in the August heat. They dropped a thousand feet and the road widened and joined the highway which ran from the Vernon Gardens across the desert to Santa Vera and the coast.

Vernon Gardens was the nearest town to the Observatory and most of it had been built within the last few years, evidently with an eye on the tourist trade. They passed a string of blue and pink-washed houses, a school constructed of glass bricks and an abstract Baptist chapel. Along the main thoroughfare the shops and stores were painted in bright jazzy colours, the vivid awnings and neon signs like street scenery in an experimental musical.

Professor Cameron turned off into a wide tree-lined square and parked by a cluster of fountains in the centre. He and Ward walked towards the cafes – Al's Fresco Diner, Ylla's, the Dome – which stretched down to the sidewalk. Around the square were a dozen gift-shops filled with cheap souvenirs: silverplate telescopes and models of the great Vernon dome masquerading as ink-stands and cigar-boxes, plus a juvenile omnium gatherum of miniature plane-taria, space helmets and plastic 3-D star atlases.

The cafe to which they went was decorated in the same futuristic motifs. The chairs and tables were painted a drab aluminium grey, their limbs and panels cut in random geometric shapes. A silver rocket ship, ten feet long, its paint peeling off in rusty strips, reared up from a pedestal among the tables. Across it was painted the cafe's name.

'The Site Tycho.'

A large mobile had been planted in the ground by the side-walk and dangled down over them, its vanes and struts flashing in the sun. Gingerly Professor Cameron pushed it away. 'I'll swear that damn thing is growing,' he confided to Ward. 'I must tell Charles to prune it.' He lowered himself into a chair by one of the open-air tables, put on a fresh pair of sunglasses and focussed them at the long brown legs of a girl sauntering past.

Left alone for the moment, Ward looked around him and picked at a cellophane transfer of a ringed planet glued to the table-top. The Site Tycho was also used as a small science fiction exchange library. A couple of metal bookstands stood outside the cafe door, where a soberly dressed middle-aged man, obviously hiding behind his upturned collar, worked his way quickly through the rows of paperbacks. At another table a young man with an intent, serious face was reading a magazine. His high cerebrotonic forehead was marked across the temple by a ridge of pink tissue, which Ward wryly decided was a lobotomy scar.

'Perhaps we ought to show our landing permits,' he said to Cameron when after three or four minutes no one had appeared to serve them. 'Or at least get our pH's checked.'

Professor Cameron grinned. 'Don't worry, no customs, no surgery.' He took his eyes off the side-walk for a moment. 'This looks like him now.'

A tall, bearded man in a short-sleeved tartan shirt and pale green slacks came out of the cafe towards them with two cups of coffee on a tray.

'Hello, Charles,' Cameron greeted him. 'There you are. We were beginning to think we'd lost ourselves in a time-trap.'

The tall man grunted something and put the cups down. Ward guessed that he was about 55 years old. He was well over six feet tall, with a massive sunburnt head and lean but powerfully muscled arms.

'Andrew, this is Charles Kandinski.' Cameron introduced the two men. 'Andrew's come to work for me, Charles. He photographed all those Cepheids for the Milan Conference last year.'

Kandinski nodded. His eyes examined Ward critically but showed no signs of interest.

'I've been telling him all about you, Charles,' Cameron went on, 'and how we all follow your work. No further news yet, I trust?'

Kandinski's lips parted in a slight smile. He listened politely to Cameron's banter and looked out over the square, his great seamed head raised to the sky.

'Andrew's read your book, Charles,' Cameron was saying. 'Very interested. He'd like to see the originals of those photographs. Wouldn't you, Andrew?'

'Yes, I certainly would,' Ward said.

Kandinski gazed down at him again. His expression was not so much penetrating as detached and impersonal, as if he were assessing Ward with an utter lack of bias, so complete, in fact, that it left no room for even the smallest illusion. Previously Ward had only seen this expression in the eyes of the very old. 'Good,' Kandinski said. 'At present they are in a safe deposit box at my bank, but if you are serious I will get them out.'

Just then two young women wearing wide-brimmed Rapallo hats made their way through the tables. They sat down and smiled at Kandinski. He nodded to Ward and Cameron and went over to the young women, who began to chatter to him animatedly.

'Well, he seems popular with them,' Ward commented. 'He's certainly not what I anticipated. I hope I didn't offend him over the plates. He was taking you seriously.'

'He's a little sensitive about them,' Cameron explained. 'The famous dustbin-lid flying saucers. You mustn't think I bait him, though. To tell the truth I hold Charles in great respect. When all's said and done, we're in the same racket.'

'Are we?' Ward said doubtfully. 'I haven't read his book. Does he say in so many words that he saw and spoke to a visitor from Venus?'

'Precisely. Don't you believe him?'

Ward laughed and looked through the coins in his pocket, leaving one on the table. 'I haven't tried to yet. You say the whole thing isn't a hoax?'

'Of course not.'

'How do you explain it then? Compensation-fantasy or – '

Professor Cameron smiled. 'Wait until you know Charles a little better.'

'I already know the man's messianic,' Ward said dryly. 'Let me guess the rest. He lives on yoghurt, weaves his own clothes, and stands on his head all night, reciting the Bhagavadgita backwards.'

'He doesn't,' Cameron said, still smiling at Ward. 'He happens to be a big man who suffers from barber's rash. I thought he'd have you puzzled.'

Ward pulled the transfer off the table. Some science fantast had skillfully pencilled in an imaginary topography on the planet's surface. There were canals, craters and lake systems named Verne, Wells and Bradbury. 'Where did he see this Venusian?' Ward asked, trying to keep the curiosity out of his voice.

'About twenty miles from here, out in the desert off the Santa Vera highway. He was picnicking with some friends, went off for a stroll in the sandhills and ran straight into the space-ship. His friends swear he was perfectly normal both immediately before and after the landing, and all of them saw the inscribed metallic tablet which the Venusian pilot left behind. Some sort of ultimatum, if I remember, warning mankind to abandon all its space programmes. Apparently someone up there does not like us.'

'Has he still got the tablet?' Ward asked.

'No. Unluckily it combusted spontaneously in the heat. But Charles managed to take a photograph of it.'

Ward laughed. 'I bet he did. It sounds like a beautifully organized hoax. I suppose he made a fortune out of his book?'

'About 150 dollars. He had to pay for the printing himself. Why do you think he works here? The reviews were too unfavourable. People who read science fiction apparently dislike flying saucers, and everyone else dismissed him as a lunatic.' He stood up. 'We might as well get back.'

As they left the cafe Cameron waved to Kandinski, who was still talking to the young women. They were leaning forward and listening with rapt attention to whatever he was saying.

'What do the people in Vernon Gardens think of him?' Ward asked as they moved away under the trees.

'Well, it's a curious thing, almost without exception those who actually know Kandinski are convinced he's sincere and that he saw an alien space craft, while at the same time realizing the absolute impossibility of the whole story.'

'"I know God exists, but I cannot *believe* in him"?'

'Exactly. Naturally, most people in Vernon think he's crazy. About three months after he met the Venusian, Charles saw another UFO chasing its tail over the town. He got the Fire Police out, alerted the Radar Command chain and even had the National Guard driving around town ringing a bell. Sure enough, there were two white blobs diving about in the clouds. Unfortunately for Charles, they were caused by the headlights of one of the asparagus farmers in the valley doing some night spraying. Charles was the first to admit it, but at 3 o'clock in the morning no one was very pleased.'

'Who is Kandinski, anyway?' Ward asked. 'Where does he come from?'

'He doesn't make a profession of seeing Venusians, if that's what you mean. He was born in Alaska, for some years taught psychology at Mexico City University. He's been just about everywhere, had a thousand different jobs. A veteran of the private evacuations. Get his book.'

Ward murmured non-committally. They entered a small arcade and stood for a moment by the first shop, an aquarium called 'The Nouvelle Vague,' watching the Angel fish and Royal Brahmins swim dreamily up and down their tanks.

'It's worth reading,' Professor Cameron went on. 'Without exaggerating, it's really one of the most interesting documents I've ever come across.'

'I'm afraid I have a closed mind when it comes to interplanetary bogey-men,' Ward said.

'A pity,' Cameron rejoined. 'I find them fascinating. Straight out of the unconscious. The fish too,' he added, pointing at the tanks. He grinned whimsically at Ward and ducked away into a horticulture store halfway down the arcade.

While Professor Cameron was looking through the sprays on the hormone counter, Ward went over to a news-stand and glanced at the magazines. The proximity of the observatory had prompted a large selection of popular astronomical guides and digests, most of them with illustrations of the Mount Vernon domes on their wrappers. Among them Ward noticed a dusty, dog-eared paperback,

'The Landings from Outer Space,' by Charles Kandinski. On the front cover a gigantic space vehicle, at least the size of New York, tens of thousands of portholes ablaze with light, was soaring majestically across a brilliant backdrop of stars and spiral nebulae.

Ward picked up the book and turned to the end cover. Here there was a photograph of Kandinski, dressed in a dark lounge suit several sizes too small, peering stiffly into the eye-piece of his MacDonald.

Ward hesitated before finally taking out his wallet. He bought the book and slipped it into his pocket as Professor Cameron emerged from the horticulture store.

'Get your shampoo?' Ward asked.

Cameron brandished a brass insecticide gun, then slung it, buccaneer-like, under his belt. 'My disintegrator,' he said, patting the butt of the gun. 'There's a positive plague of white ants in the garden, like something out of a science fiction nightmare. I've tried to convince Edna that their real source is psychological. Remember the story "Leiningen vs the Ants"? A classic example of the forces of the Id rebelling against the Super-Ego.' He watched a girl in a black bikini and lemon-coloured sunglasses move gracefully through the arcade and added meditatively: 'You know, Andrew, like everyone else my real vocation was to be a psychiatrist. I spend so long analysing my motives I've no time left to act.'

'Kandinski's Super-Ego must be in difficulties,' Ward remarked. 'You haven't told me your explanation yet.'

'What explanation?'

'Well, what's really at the bottom of this Venusian he claims to have seen?'

'Nothing is at the bottom of it. Why?'

Ward smiled helplessly. 'You will tell me next that you really believe him.'

Professor Cameron chuckled. They reached his car and climbed in. 'Of course I do,' he said.

When, three days later, Ward borrowed Professor Cameron's car and drove down to the rail depot in Vernon Gardens to collect a case of slides which had followed him across the Atlantic, he had no intention of seeing Charles Kandinski again. He had read one or two chapters of Kandinski's book before going to sleep the previous night and dropped it in boredom. Kandinski's description of his encounter with the Venusian was not only puerile and crudely

89

written but, most disappointing of all, completely devoid of imagination. Ward's work at the Institute was now taking up most of his time. The Annual Congress of the International Geophysical Association was being held at Mount Vernon in little under a month, and most of the burden for organizing the three-week program of lectures, semesters and dinners had fallen on Professor Cameron and himself.

But as he drove away from the depot past the cafes in the square he caught sight of Kandinski on the terrace of the Site Tycho. It was 3 o'clock, a time when most people in Vernon Gardens were lying asleep indoors, and Kandinski seemed to be the only person out in the sun. He was scrubbing away energetically at the abstract tables with his long hairy arms, head down so that his beard was almost touching the metal tops, like an aboriginal halfman prowling in dim bewilderment over the ruins of a futuristic city lost in an inversion of time.

On an impulse, Ward parked the car in the square and walked across to the Site Tycho, but as soon as Kandinski came over to his table he wished he had gone to another of the cafes. Kandinski had been reticent enough the previous day, but now that Cameron was absent he might well turn out to be a garrulous bore.

After serving him Kandinski sat down on a bench by the bookshelves and stared moodily at his feet. Ward watched him quietly for five minutes, as the mobiles revolved delicately in the warm air, deciding whether to approach Kandinski. Then he stood up and went over to the rows of magazines. He picked in a desultory way through half a dozen and turned to Kandinski. 'Can you recommend any of these?'

Kandinski looked up. 'Do you read science fiction?' he asked matter-of-factly.

'Not as a rule,' Ward admitted. When Kandinski said nothing he went on: 'Perhaps I'm too sceptical, but I can't take it seriously.'

Kandinski pulled a blister on his palm. 'No one suggests you should. What you mean is that you take it too seriously.'

Accepting the rebuke with a smile at himself, Ward pulled out one of the magazines and sat down at a table next to Kandinski. On the cover was a placid suburban setting of snugly eaved houses, yew trees and children's bicycles. Spreading slowly across the roof-tops was an enormous pulpy nightmare, blocking out the sun behind it and throwing a weird phosphorescent glow over the roofs and lawns.

90

'You're probably right,' Ward said, showing the cover to Kandinski. 'I'd hate to want to take that seriously.'

Kandinski waved it aside. 'I have seen 11th century illuminations of the pentateuch more sensational than any of these covers.' He pointed to the cinema theatre on the far side of the square, where the four-hour Biblical epic "Cain and Abel" was showing. Above the trees an elaborate technicolored hoarding showed Cain, wearing what appeared to be a suit of Roman armour, wrestling with an immense hydraheaded boa constrictor.

Kandinski shrugged tolerantly. 'If Michelangelo were working for MGM today would he produce anything better?'

Ward laughed. 'You may well be right. Perhaps the House of the Medicis should be re-christened "16th Century-Fox"'

Kandinski stood up and straightened the shelves. 'I saw you here with Godfrey Cameron,' he said over his shoulder. 'You're working at the Observatory?'

'At the Hubble.'

Kandinski came and sat down beside Ward. 'Cameron is a good man. A very pleasant fellow.'

'He thinks a great deal of you,' Ward volunteered, realizing that Kandinski was probably short of friends.

'You mustn't believe everything that Cameron says about me,' Kandinski said suddenly. He hesitated, apparently uncertain whether to confide further in Ward, and then took the magazine from him. 'There are better ones here. You have to exercise some discrimination.'

'It's not so much the sensationalism that puts me off,' Ward explained, 'as the psychological implications. Most of the themes in these stories come straight out of the more unpleasant reaches of the unconscious.'

Kandinski glanced sharply at Ward, a trace of amusement in his eyes. 'That sounds rather dubious and, if I may say so, second-hand. Take the best of these stories for what they are: imaginative exercises on the theme of tomorrow.'

'You read a good deal of science fiction?' Ward asked.

Kandinski shook his head. 'Never. Not since I was a child.'

'I'm surprised' Ward said. 'Professor Cameron told me you had written a science fiction novel.'

'Not a novel,' Kandinski corrected.

'I'd like to read it,' Ward went on. 'From what Cameron said it sounded fascinating, almost Swiftian in concept. This spacecraft which arrives from Venus and the strange conversations the pilot holds with a philosopher he meets. A modern morality. Is that the subject?'

Kandinski watched Ward thoughtfully before replying. 'Loosely, yes. But, as I said, the book is not a novel. It is a factual and literal report of a Venus landing which actually took place, a diary of the most significant encounter in history since Paul saw his vision of Christ on the road to Damascus.' He lifted his huge bearded head and gazed at Ward without embarrassment. 'As a matter of interest, as Professor Cameron probably explained to you, I was the man who witnessed the landing.'

Still maintaining his pose, Ward frowned intently. 'Well, in fact Cameron did say something of the sort, but I . . .'

'But you found it difficult to believe?' Kandinski suggested ironically.

'Just a little,' Ward admitted. 'Are you seriously claiming that you did see a Venusian space-craft?'

Kandinski nodded. 'Exactly.' Then, as if aware that their conversation had reached a familiar turning he suddenly seemed to lose interest in Ward. 'Excuse me.' He nodded politely to Ward, picked up a length of hose-pipe connected to a faucet and began to spray one of the big mobiles.

Puzzled but still sceptical, Ward sat back and watched him critically, then fished in his pockets for some change. 'I must say I admire you for taking it all so calmly,' he told Kandinski as he paid him.

'What makes you think I do?'

'Well, if I'd seen, let alone spoken to a visitor from Venus I think I'd be running around in a flat spin, notifying every government and observatory in the world.'

'I did,' Kandinski said. 'As far as I could. No one was very interested.'

Ward shook his head and laughed. 'It is incredible, to put it mildly.'

'I agree with you.'

'What I mean,' Ward said, 'is that it's straight out of one of these science fiction stories of yours.'

Kandinski rubbed his lips with a scarred knuckle, obviously

searching for some means of ending the conversation. 'The resemblance is misleading. They are not my stories,' he added parenthetically. 'This cafe is the only one which would give me work, for a perhaps obvious reason. As for the incredibility, let me say that I was and still am completely amazed. You may think I take it all calmly, but ever since the landing I have lived in a state of acute anxiety and foreboding. But short of committing some spectacular crime to draw attention to myself I don't see now how I can convince anyone.'

Ward gestured with his glasses. 'Perhaps. But I'm surprised you don't realize the very simple reasons why people refuse to take you seriously. For example, why should you be the only person to witness an event of such staggering implications? Why have *you* alone seen a Venusian?'

'A sheer accident.'

'But why should a space craft from Venus land here?'

'What better place than near Mount Vernon Observatory?'

'I can think of any number. The UN Assembly, for one.'

Kandinski smiled lightly. 'Columbus didn't make his first contacts with the North-American Indians at the Iroquois-Sioux Tribal Conference.'

'That may be,' Ward admitted, beginning to feel impatient. 'What did this Venusian look like?'

Kandinski smiled wearily at the empty tables and picked up his hose again. 'I don't know whether you've read my book,' he said, 'but if you haven't you'll find it all there.'

'Professor Cameron mentioned that you took some photographs of the Venusian space-craft. Could I examine them?'

'Certainly,' Kandinski replied promptly. 'I'll bring them here tomorrow. You're welcome to test them in any way you wish.'

That evening Ward had dinner with the Camerons. Professor Renthall, Director of the Hubble, and his wife completed the party. The table-talk consisted almost entirely of good-humoured gossip about their colleagues retailed by Cameron and Renthall, and Ward was able to mention his conversation with Kandinski.

'At first I thought he was mad, but now I'm not so certain. There's something rather too subtle about him. The way he creates an impression of absolute integrity, but at the same time never gives you a chance to tackle him directly on any point of detail. And when you do manage to ask him outright about this Venusian his answers are far too pat. I'm convinced the whole thing is an elaborate hoax.'

Professor Renthall shook his head. 'No, it's no hoax. Don't you agree, Godfrey?'

Cameron nodded. 'Not in Andrew's sense, anyway.'

'But what other explanation is there?' Ward asked. 'We know he hasn't seen a Venusian, so he must be a fraud. Unless you think he's a lunatic. And he certainly doesn't behave like one.'

'What is a lunatic?' Professor Renthall asked rhetorically, peering into the faceted stem of his raised hock glass. 'Merely a man with more understanding than he can contain. I think Charles belongs in that category.'

'The definition doesn't explain him, sir,' Ward insisted. 'He's going to lend me his photographs and when I prove those are fakes I think I'll be able to get under his guard.'

'Poor Charles,' Edna Cameron said. 'Why shouldn't he have seen a space ship? I think I see them every day.'

'That's just what I feel, dear,' Cameron said, patting his wife's matronly, brocaded shoulder. 'Let Charles have his Venusian if he wants to. Damn it, all it's trying to do is ban Project Apollo. An excellent idea, I have always maintained; only the professional astronomer has any business in space. After the Rainbow tests there isn't an astronomer anywhere in the world who wouldn't follow Charles Kandinski to the stake.' He turned to Renthall. 'By the way, I wonder what Charles is planning for the Congress? A Neptunian? Or perhaps a whole delegation from Proxima Centauri. We ought to fit him out with a space suit and a pavilion – "Charles Kandinski – New Worlds for Old".'

'Santa Claus in a space-suit,' Professor Renthall mused. 'That's a new one. Send him a ticket.'

The next weekend Ward returned the twelve plates to the Site Tycho.

'Well?' Kandinski asked.

'It's difficult to say,' Ward answered. 'They're all too heavily absorbed. They could be clever montages of light brackets and turbine blades. One of them looks like a close-up of a clutch plate. There's a significant lack of any real corroborative details which you'd expect somewhere in so wide a selection.' He paused. 'On the other hand, they could be genuine.'

Kandinski said nothing, took the paper package, and went off into the cafe.

The interior of the Site Tycho had been designed to represent the control room of a space-ship on the surface of the Moon. Hidden fluorescent lighting glimmered through plastic wall fascia and filled the room with an eerie blue glow. Behind the bar a large mural threw the curving outline of the Moon on to an illuminated star-scape. The doors leading to the rest-rooms were circular and bulged outwards like air-locks, distinguished from each other by the symbols ♂ and ♀. The total effect was ingenious but somehow reminiscent to Ward of a twenty-fifth century cave.

He sat down at the bar and waited while Kandinski packed the plates away carefully in an old leather brief-case.

'I've read your book,' Ward said. 'I had looked at it the last time I saw you, but I read it again thoroughly.' He waited for some comment upon this admission, but Kandinski went over to an old portable typewriter standing at the far end of the bar and began to type laboriously with one finger. 'Have you seen any more Venusians since the book was published?' Ward asked.

'None,' Kandinski said.

'Do you think you will?'

'Perhaps.' Kandinski shrugged and went on with his typing.

'What are you working on now?' Ward asked.

'A lecture I am giving on Friday evening,' Kandinski said. Two keys locked together and he flicked them back. 'Would you care to come? Eight-thirty, at the high school near the Baptist chapel.'

'If I can,' Ward said. He saw that Kandinski wanted to get rid of him. 'Thanks for letting me see the plates.' He made his way out into the sun. People were walking about through the fresh morning air, and he caught the clean scent of peach blossom carried down the slopes into the town.

Suddenly Ward felt how enclosed and insane it had been inside the Tycho, and how apposite had been his description of it as a cave, with its residential magician incanting over his photographs like a down-at-heel Merlin manipulating his set of runes. He felt annoyed with himself for becoming involved with Kandinski and allowing the potent charisma of his personality to confuse him. Obviously Kandinski played upon the instinctive sympathy for the outcast, his whole pose of integrity and conviction a device for drawing the gullible towards him.

Letting the light spray from the fountains fall across his face, Ward crossed the square towards his car.

Away in the distance 2,000 feet above, rising beyond a screen of fir trees, the three Mount Vernon domes shone together in the sun like a futuristic Taj Mahal.

Fifteen miles from Vernon Gardens the Santa Vera highway circled down from the foot of Mount Vernon into the first low scrub-covered hills which marked the southern edge of the desert. Ward looked out at the long banks of coarse sand stretching away through the haze, their outlines blurring in the afternoon heat. He glanced at the book lying on the seat beside him, open at the map printed between its end covers, and carefully checked his position, involuntarily slowing the speed of the Chevrolet as he moved nearer to the site of the Venus landings.

In the fortnight since he had returned the photographs to the Site Tycho, he had seen Kandinski only once, at the lecture delivered the previous night. Ward had deliberately stayed away from the Site Tycho, but he had seen a poster advertising the lecture and driven down to the school despite himself.

The lecture was delivered in the gymnasium before an audience of forty or fifty people, most of them women, who formed one of the innumerable local astronomical societies. Listening to the talk round him, Ward gathered that their activities principally consisted of trying to identify more than half a dozen of the constellations. Kandinski had lectured to them on several occasions and the subject of this latest instalment was his researches into the significance of the Venusian tablet he had been analysing for the last three years.

When Kandinski stepped onto the dais there was a brief round of applause. He was wearing a lounge suit of a curiously archaic cut and had washed his beard, which bushed out above his string tie so that he resembled a Mormon patriarch or the homespun saint of some fervent evangelical community.

For the benefit of any new members, he prefaced his lecture with a brief account of his meeting with the Venusian, and then turned to his analysis of the tablet. This was the familiar ultimatum warning mankind to abandon its preparations for the exploration of space, for the ostensible reason that, just as the sea was a universal image of the unconscious, so space was nothing less than an image of psychosis and death, and that if he tried to penetrate the interplanetary voids man would only plunge to earth like a demented Icarus, unable to scale the vastness of the cosmic zero. Kandinski's real motives for introducing this were all too apparent – the expected success of Project Apollo and subsequent landings on Mars and Venus would, if nothing else, conclusively expose his fantasies.

However, by the end of the lecture Ward found that his opinion of Kandinski had experienced a complete about face.

As a lecturer Kandinski was poor, losing words, speaking in a slow ponderous style and trapping himself in long subordinate clauses, but his quiet, matter-of-fact tone and absolute conviction in the importance of what he was saying, coupled with the nature of his material, held the talk together. His analysis of the Venusian cryptograms, a succession of intricate philological theorems, was well above the heads of his audience, but what began to impress Ward, as much as the painstaking preparation which must have preceded the lecture, was Kandinski's acute nervousness in delivering it. Ward noticed that he suffered from an irritating speech impediment that made it difficult for him to pronounce 'Venusian', and he saw that Kandinski, far from basking in the limelight, was delivering the lecture only out of a deep sense of obligation to his audience and was greatly relieved when the ordeal was over.

At the end Kandinski had invited questions. These, with the exception of the chairman's, all concerned the landing of the alien space vehicle and ignored the real subject of the lecture. Kandinski answered them all carefully, taking in good part the inevitable facetious questions. Ward noted with interest the audience's curious ambivalence, simultaneously fascinated by and resentful of Kandinski's exposure of their own private fantasies, an expression of the same ambivalence which had propelled so many of the mana-personalities of history towards their inevitable Calvarys.

Just as the chairman was about to close the meeting, Ward stood up.

'Mr Kandinski. You say that this Venusian indicated that there was also life on one of the moons of Uranus. Can you tell us how he did this if there was no verbal communication between you?'

Kandinski showed no surprise at seeing Ward. 'Certainly; as I told you, he drew eight concentric circles in the sand, one for each of the planets. Around Uranus he drew five lesser orbits and marked one of these. Then he pointed to himself and to me and to a patch of lichen. From this I deduced, reasonably I maintain, that –'

'Excuse me, Mr Kandinski,' Ward interrupted. 'You say he drew five orbits around Uranus? One for each of the moons?'

Kandinski nodded. 'Yes. Five.'

'That was in 1960,' Ward went on. 'Three weeks ago Professor Pineau at Brussels discovered a sixth moon of Uranus.'

The audience looked around at Ward and began to murmur.

'Why should this Venusian have omitted one of the moons?' Ward asked, his voice ringing across the gymnasium.

Kandinski frowned and peered at Ward suspiciously. 'I didn't know there was a sixth moon . . . ' he began.

'Exactly!' someone called out. The audience began to titter.

'I can understand the Venusian not wishing to introduce any difficulties,' Ward said, 'but this seems a curious way of doing it.'

Kandinski appeared at a loss. Then he introduced Ward to the audience. 'Dr Ward is a professional while I am only an amateur,' he admitted. 'I am afraid I cannot explain the anomaly. Perhaps my memory is at fault. But I am sure the Venusian drew only five orbits.' He stepped down from the dais and strode out hurriedly, scowling into his beard, pursued by a few derisory hoots from the audience.

It took Ward fifteen minutes to free himself from the knot of admiring white-gloved spinsters who cornered him between two vaulting horses. When he broke away he ran out to his car and drove into Vernon Gardens, hoping to see Kandinski and apologize to him.

Five miles into the desert Ward approached a nexus of rock-cuttings and causeways which were part of an abandoned irrigation scheme. The colours of the hills were more vivid now, bright siliconic reds and yellows, crossed with sharp stabs of light from the exposed quartz veins. Following the map on the seat, he turned off the highway onto a rough track which ran along the bank of a dried-up canal. He passed a few rusting sections of picket fencing, a derelict grader half-submerged under the sand, and a collection of dilapidated metal shacks. The car bumped over the potholes at little more than ten miles an hour, throwing up clouds of hot ashy dust that swirled high into the air behind him.

Two miles along the canal the track came to an end. Ward stopped the car and waited for the dust to subside. Carrying Kandinski's book in front of him like a divining instrument, he set off on foot across the remaining three hundred yards. The contours around him were marked on the map, but the hills had shifted several hundred yards westwards since the book's publication and he found himself wandering about from one crest to another, peering into shallow depressions only as old as the last sand-storm. The entire landscape seemed haunted by strange currents and moods; the sand swirls surging down the aisles of dunes and the proximity of the horizon enclosed the whole place of stones with invisible walls.

Finally he found the ring of hills indicated and climbed a narrow saddle leading to its centre. When he scaled the thirty-foot slope he stopped abruptly.

Down on his knees in the middle of the basin with his back to Ward, the studs of his boots flashing in the sunlight, was Kandinski. There was a clutter of tiny objects on the sand around him, and at first Ward thought he was at prayer, making his oblations to the tutelary deities of Venus. Then he saw that Kandinski was slowly scraping the surface of the ground with a small trowel. A circle about 20 yards in diameter had been marked off with pegs and string into a series of wedge-shaped allotments. Every few seconds Kandinski carefully decanted a small heap of grit into one of the test-tubes mounted in a wooden rack in front of him.

Ward put away the book and walked down the slope. Kandinski looked around and then climbed to his feet. The coating of red ash on his beard gave him a fiery, prophetic look. He recognized Ward and raised the trowel in greeting.

Ward stopped at the edge of the string perimeter. 'What on earth are you doing?'

'I am collecting soil specimens.' Kandinski bent down and corked one of the tubes. He looked tired but worked away steadily.

Ward watched him finish a row. 'It's going to take you a long time to cover the whole area. I thought there weren't any gaps left in the Periodic Table.'

'The space-craft rotated at speed before it rose into the air. This surface is abrasive enough to have scratched off a few minute filings. With luck I may find one of them.' Kandinski smiled thinly. '262. Venusium, I hope.'

Ward started to say: 'But the transuranic elements decay spontaneously . . . ' and then walked over to the centre of the circle, where there was a round indentation, three feet deep and five across. The inner surface was glazed and smooth. It was shaped like an inverted cone and looked as if it had been caused by the boss of an enormous spinning top. 'This is where the space-craft landed?'

Kandinski nodded. He filled the last tube and then stowed the rack away in a canvas satchel. He came over to Ward and stared down at the hole. 'What does it look like to you? A meteor impact? Or an oil drill, perhaps?' A smile showed behind his dusty beard. 'The F-109's at the Air Force Weapons School begin their target runs across here. It might have been caused by a rogue cannon shell.'

Ward stooped down and felt the surface of the pit, running his fingers thoughtfully over the warm fused silica. 'More like a 500-pound bomb. But the cone is geometrically perfect. It's certainly unusual.'

'Unusual?' Kandinski chuckled to himself and picked up the satchel.

'Has anyone else been out here?' Ward asked as they trudged up the slope.

'Two so-called experts.' Kandinski slapped the sand off his knees. 'A geologist from Gulf-Vacuum and an Air Force ballistics officer. You'll be glad to hear that they both thought I had dug the pit myself and then fused the surface with an acetylene torch.' He peered critically at Ward. 'Why did you come out here today?'

'Idle curiosity,' Ward said. 'I had an afternoon off and I felt like a drive.'

They reached the crest of the hill and he stopped and looked down into the basin. The lines of string split the circle into a strange horological device, a huge zodiacal mandala, the dark patches in the arcs Kandinski had been working telling its stations.

'You were going to tell me why you came out here,' Kandinski said as they walked back to the car.

Ward shrugged. 'I suppose I wanted to prove something to myself. There's a problem of reconciliation.' He hesitated, and then began: 'You see, there are some things which are self-evidently false. The laws of common sense and everyday experience refute them. I know a lot of the evidence for many things we believe in is pretty thin, but I don't have to embark on a theory of knowledge to decide that the Moon isn't made of green cheese.'

'Well?' Kandinski shifted the satchel to his other shoulder.

'This Venusian you've seen,' Ward said. 'The landing, the runic tablet. I can't believe them. Every piece of evidence I've seen, all the

100

circumstantial details, the facts given in this book . . . they're all patently false.' He turned to one of the middle chapters. 'Take this at random – "A phosphorescent green fluid pulsed through the dorsal lung-chamber of the Prime's helmet, inflating two opaque fan-like gills . . . "' Ward closed the book and shrugged helplessly. Kandinski stood a few feet away from him, the sunlight breaking across the deep lines of his face.

'Now I know what you say to my objections,' Ward went on. 'If you told a 19th century chemist that lead could be transmuted into gold he would have dismissed you as a mediaevalist. But the point is that he'd have been right to do so – '

'I understand,' Kandinski interrupted. 'But you still haven't explained why you came out here today.'

Ward stared out over the desert. High above, a stratojet was doing cuban eights into the sun, the spiral vapour trails drifting across the sky like gigantic fragments of an apocalyptic message. Looking around, he realized that Kandinski must have walked from the bus-stop on the highway. 'I'll give you a lift back,' he said.

As they drove along the canal he turned to Kandinski. 'I enjoyed your lecture last night. I apologize for trying to make you look a fool.'

Kandinski was loosening his boot-straps. He laughed unreproach-fully. 'You put me in an awkward position. I could hardly have challenged you. I can't afford to subscribe to every astronomical journal. Though a sixth moon would have been big news.' As they neared Vernon Gardens he asked: 'Would you like to come in and look at the tablet analysis?'

Ward made no reply to the invitation. He drove around the square and parked under the trees, then looked up at the fountains, tapping his fingers on the wind-shield. Kandinski sat beside him, cogitating into his beard.

Ward watched him carefully. 'Do you think this Venusian will return?'

Kandinski nodded. 'Yes. I am sure he will.'

Later they sat together at a broad roll-top desk in the room above the Tycho. Around the wall hung white cardboard screens packed with lines of cuneiform glyphics and Kandinski's progressive breakdown of their meaning.

Ward held an enlargement of the original photograph of the Venusian tablet and listened to Kandinski's explanation.

'As you see from this,' Kandinski explained, 'in all probability there are not millions of Venusians, as every one would expect, but only three or four of them altogether. Two are circling Venus, a third Uranus and possibly a fourth is in orbit around Neptune. This solves the difficulty that puzzled you and antagonizes everyone else. Why should the Prime have approached only one person out of several hundred million and selected him on a completely random basis? Now obviously he had seen the Russian and American satellite capsules and asssumed that our race, like his now, numbered no more than three or four, then concluded from the atmospheric H-bomb tests that we were in conflict and would soon destroy ourselves. This is one of the reasons why I think he will return shortly and why it is important to organize a world-wide reception for him on a governmental level.'

'Wait a minute,' Ward said. 'He must have known that the population of this planet numbered more than three or four. Even the weakest telescope would demonstrate that.'

'Of course, but he would naturally assume that the millions of inhabitants of the Earth belonged to an aboriginal sub-species, perhaps employed as work animals. After all, if he observed that despite this planet's immense resources the bulk of its population lived like animals, an alien visitor could only decide that they were considered as such.'

'But space vehicles are supposed to have been observing us since the Babylonian era, long before the development of satellite rockets. There have been thousands of recorded sightings.'

Kandinski shook his head. 'None of them has been authenticated.'

'What about the other landings that have been reported recently?' Ward asked. 'Any number of people have seen Venusians and Martians.'

'Have they?' Kandinski asked sceptically. 'I wish I could believe that. Some of the encounters reveal marvellous powers of invention, but no one can accept them as anything but fantasy.'

'The same criticism has been levelled at your spacecraft,' Ward reminded him.

Kandinski seemed to lose patience. 'I *saw* it,' he explained, impotently tossing his notebook on to the desk. 'I *spoke* to the Prime!'

Ward nodded non-committally and picked up the photograph again. Kandinski stepped over to him and took it out of his hands.

'Ward,' he said carefully. 'Believe me. You must. You know I am too big a man to waste myself on a senseless charade.' His massive hands squeezed Ward's shoulder, and almost lifted him off the seat. '*Believe* me. Together we can be ready for the next landings and alert the world. I am only Charles Kandinski, a waiter at a third-rate cafe, but you are Dr Andrew Ward of Mount Vernon Observatory. They will listen to you. Try to realize what this may mean for mankind.'

Ward pulled himself away from Kandinski and rubbed his shoulders.

'Ward, do you believe me? Ask yourself.'

Ward looked up pensively at Kandinski towering over him, his red beard like the burning, unconsumed bush.

'I think so,' he said quietly. 'Yes, I do.'

A week later the 23rd Congress of the International Geophysical Association opened at Mount Vernon Observatory. At 3.30 P.M., in the Hoyle Library amphitheatre, Professor Renthall was to deliver the inaugural address welcoming the 92 delegates and 25 newspaper and agency reporters to the fortnight's programme of lectures and discussions.

Shortly after 11 o'clock that morning Ward and Professor Cameron completed their final arrangements and escaped down to Vernon Gardens for an hour's relaxation.

'Well,' Cameron said as they walked over to the Site Tycho, 'I've got a pretty good idea of what it must be like to run the Waldorf-Astoria.' They picked one of the sidewalk tables and sat down. 'I haven't been here for weeks,' Cameron said. 'How are you getting on with the Man in the Moon?'

'Kandinski? I hardly ever see him,' Ward said.

'I was talking to the *Time* magazine stringer about Charles,' Cameron said, cleaning his sunglasses. 'He thought he might do a piece about him.'

'Hasn't Kandinski suffered enough of that sort of thing?' Ward asked moodily.

'Perhaps he has,' Cameron agreed. 'Is he still working on his crossword puzzle? The tablet thing, whatever he calls it.'

Casually, Ward said: 'He has a theory that it should be possible to see the lunar bases. Refuelling points established there by the Venusians over the centuries.'

'Interesting,' Cameron commented.

'They're sited near Copernicus,' Ward went on. 'I know Vandone

103

at Milan is mapping Archimedes and the Imbrium, I thought I might mention it to him at his semester tomorrow.'

Professor Cameron took off his glasses and gazed quizzically at Ward. 'My dear Andrew, what has been going on? Don't tell me you've become one of Charles' converts?'

Ward laughed and shook his head. 'Of course not. Obviously there are no lunar bases or alien space craft. I don't for a moment believe a word Kandinski says.' He gestured helplessly. 'At the same time I admit I have become involved with him. There's something about Kandinski's personality. On the one hand I can't take him seriously – '

'Oh, I take him seriously,' Cameron cut in smoothly. 'Very seriously indeed, if not quite in the sense you mean.' Cameron turned his back on the sidewalk crowds. 'Jung's views on flying saucers are very illuminating, Andrew; they'd help you to understand Kandinski. Jung believes that civilization now stands at the conclusion of a Platonic Great Year, at the eclipse of the sign of Pisces which has dominated the Christian epoch, and that we are entering the sign of Aquarius, a period of confusion and psychic chaos. He remarks that throughout history, at all times of uncertainty and discord, cosmic space vehicles have been seen approaching Earth, and that in a few extreme cases actual meetings with their occupants are supposed to have taken place.'

As Cameron paused, Ward glanced across the tables for Kandinski, but a relief waiter served them and he assumed it was Kandinski's day off.

Cameron continued: 'Most people regard Charles Kandinski as a lunatic, but as a matter of fact he is performing one of the most important roles in the world today, the role of a prophet alerting people of this coming crisis. The real significance of his fantasies, like that of the ban-the-bomb movements, is to be found elsewhere than on the conscious plane, as an expression of the immense psychic forces stirring below the surface of rational life, like the isotactic movements of the continental tables which heralded the major geological transformations.'

Ward shook his head dubiously. 'I can accept that a man such as Freud was a prophet, but Charles Kandinski – ?'

'Certainly. Far more than Freud. It's unfortunate for Kandinski, and for the writers of science fiction for that matter, that they have to

104

perform their tasks of describing the symbols of transformation in a so-called rationalist society, where a scientific, or at least a pesudo-scientific explanation is required *a priori*. And because the true prophet never deals in what may be rationally deduced, people such as Charles are ignored or derided today.'

'It's interesting that Kandinski compared his meeting with the Venusian with Paul's conversion on the road to Damascus,' Ward said.

'He was quite right. In both encounters you see the same mechanism of blinding unconscious revelation. And you can see too that Charles feels the same overwelming need to spread the Pauline revelation to the world. The Anti-Apollo movement is only now getting under way, but within the next decade it will recruit millions, and men such as Charles Kandinski will be the fathers of its apocalypse.'

'You make him sound like a titanic figure,' Ward remarked quietly. 'I think he's just a lonely, tired man obsessed by something he can't understand. Perhaps he simply needs a few friends to confide in.'

Slowly shaking his head, Cameron tapped the table with his glasses. 'Be warned, Andrew, you'll burn your fingers if you play with Charles' brand of fire. The mana-personalities of history have no time for personal loyalties – the founder of the Christian church made that pretty plain.'

Shortly after seven o'clock that evening Charles Kandinski mounted his bicycle and set off out of Vernon Gardens. The small room in the seedy area where he lived always depressed him on his free days from the Tycho, and as he pedalled along he ignored the shouts from his neighbours sitting out on their balconies with their crates of beer. He knew that his beard and the high, ancient bicycle with its capacious wicker basket made him a grotesque, Quixotic figure, but he felt too preoccupied to care. That morning he had heard that the French translation of 'The Landings from Outer Space', printed at his own cost, had been completely ignored by the Paris press. In addition a jobbing printer in Santa Vera was pressing him for payment for 5,000 anti-Apollo leaflets that had been distributed the previous year.

Above all had come the news on the radio that the target date of the first manned Moon flight had been advanced to 1969, and on the following day would take place the latest and most ambitious of the instrumented lunar flights. The anticipated budget for the Apollo programme (in a moment of grim humour he had calculated that it would pay for the printing of some 1,000 billion leaflets) seemed to double each year, but so far he had found little success in his attempt to alert people to the folly of venturing into space. All that day he had felt sick with frustration and anger.

At the end of the avenue he turned on to the highway which served the asparagus farms lying in the 20-mile strip between Vernon Gardens and the desert. It was a hot empty evening and few cars or trucks passed him. On either side of the road the great lemon-green terraces of asparagus lay seeping in their moist paddy beds, and occasionally a marsh-hen clacked overhead and dived out of sight.

Five miles along the road he reached the last farmhouse above the edge of the desert. He cycled on to where the road ended 200 yards ahead, dismounted and left the bicycle in a culvert. Slinging his camera over one shoulder, he walked off across the hard ground into the mouth of a small valley.

The boundary between the desert and the farm-strip was irregular. On his left, beyond the rocky slopes, he could hear a motor-reaper purring down one of the mile-long spits of fertile land running into the desert, but the barren terrain and the sense of isolation began to relax him and he forgot the irritations that had plagued him all day.

A keen naturalist, he saw a long-necked sand-crane perched on a spur of shale fifty feet from him and stopped and raised his camera. Peering through the finder he noticed that the light had faded too deeply for a photograph. Curiously, the sand-crane was clearly silhouetted against a circular glow of light which emanated from beyond a low ridge at the end of the valley. This apparently sourceless corona fitfully illuminated the darkening air, as if coming from a lighted mineshaft.

Putting away his camera, Kandinski walked forward, within a few minutes reached the ridge, and began to climb it. The face sloped steeply, and he pulled himself up by the hefts of brush and scrub, kicking away footholds in the rocky surface.

Just before he reached the crest he felt his heart surge painfully with the exertion, and he lay still for a moment, a sudden feeling of dizziness spinning in his head. He waited until the spasm subsided, shivering faintly in the cool air, an unfamiliar undertone of uneasiness in his mind. The air seemed to vibrate strangely with an intense inaudible music that pressed upon his temples. Rubbing his forehead, he lifted himself over the crest.

The ridge he had climbed was U-shaped and about 200 feet across, its open end away from him. Resting on the sandy floor in its centre was an enormous metal disc, over 100 feet in diameter and 30 feet high. It seemed to be balanced on a huge conical boss, half of which had already sunk into the sand. A fluted rim ran around the edge of the disc and separated the upper and lower curvatures, which were revolving rapidly in opposite directions, throwing off magnificent flashes of silver light.

Kandinski lay still, as his first feeling of fear retreated and his courage and presence of mind returned. The inaudible piercing music had faded, and his mind felt brilliantly clear. His eyes ran rapidly over the space-ship, and he estimated that it was over twice the size of the craft he had seen three years earlier. There were no markings or ports on the carapace, but he was certain it had not come from Venus.

Kandinski lay watching the space-craft for ten minutes, trying to decide upon his best course of action. Unfortunately he had smashed the lens of his camera. Finally, pushing himself backwards, he slid slowly down the slope. When he reached the floor he could still hear the whine of the rotors. Hiding in the pools of shadow, he made his way up the valley, and two hundred yards from the ridge he broke into a run.

He returned the way he had come, his great legs carrying him across the ruts and boulders, seized his bicycle from the culvert and pedalled rapidly towards the farmhouse.

A single light shone in an upstairs room and he pressed one hand to the bell and pounded on the screen door with the other, nearly tearing it from its hinges. Eventually a young woman appeared. She came down the stairs reluctantly, uncertain what to make of Kandinski's beard and ragged, dusty clothes.

'Telephone!' Kandinski bellowed at her, gasping wildly, as he caught back his breath.

The girl at last unlatched the door and backed away from him nervously. Kandinski lurched past her and staggered blindly around the darkened hall. 'Where is it?' he roared.

The girl switched on the lights and pointed into the sitting room. Kandinski pushed past her and rushed over to it.

Ward played with his brandy glass and discreetly loosened the collar of his dress shirt, listening to Dr MacIntyre of Greenwich Observatory, four seats away on his right, make the third of the after-dinner speeches. Ward was to speak next, and he ran through the opening phrases of his speech, glancing down occasionally to con his notes. At 34 he was the youngest member to address the Congress banquet, and by no means unimpressed by the honour. He looked at the venerable figures to his left and right at the top table, their black jackets, and white shirt fronts reflected in the table silver, and saw Professor Cameron wink at him reassuringly.

He was going through his notes for the last time when a steward bent over his shoulder. 'Telephone for you, Dr Ward.'

'I can't take it now,' Ward whispered. 'Tell them to call later.'

'The caller said it was extremely urgent, Doctor. Something about some people from the Neptune arriving.'

'The Neptune?'

'I think that's a hotel in Santa Vera. Maybe the Russian delegates have turned up after all.'

Ward pushed his chair back, made his apologies and slipped away.

Professor Cameron was waiting in the alcove outside the banqueting hall when Ward stepped out of the booth. 'Anything the trouble, Andrew? It's not your father, I hope – '

'It's Kandinski,' Ward said hurriedly. 'He's out in the desert, near the farm-strip. He says he's seen another space vehicle.'

'Oh, is that all.' Cameron shook his head. 'Come on, we'd better get back. The poor fool!'

'Hold on,' Ward said. 'He's got it under observation now. It's on the ground. He told me to call General Wayne at the air base and alert the Strategic Air Command.' Ward chewed his lip. 'I don't know what to do.'

Cameron took him by the arm. 'Andrew, come on. MacIntyre's winding up.'

'What can we do, though?' Ward asked. 'He seemed all right, but then he said that he thought they were hostile. That sounds a little sinister.'

'Andrew!' Cameron snapped. 'What's the matter with you?

108

Leave Kandinski to himself. You can't go now. It would be unpardonable rudeness.'

'I've got to help Kandinski,' Ward insisted. 'I'm sure he needs it this time.' He wrenched himself away from Cameron.

'Ward!' Professor Cameron called. 'For God's sake, come back!' He followed Ward onto the balcony and watched him run down the steps and disappear across the lawn into the darkness.

As the wheels of the car thudded over the deep ruts, Ward cut the headlights and searched the dark hills which marked the desert's edge. The warm glitter of Vernon Gardens lay behind him and only a few isolated lights shone in the darkness on either side of the road. He passed the farmhouse from which he assumed Kandinski had telephoned, then drove on slowly until he saw the bicycle Kandinski had left for him.

It took him several minutes to mount the huge machine, his feet well clear of the pedals for most of their stroke. Laboriously he covered a hundred yards, and after careering helplessly into a clump of scrub was forced to dismount and continue on foot.

Kandinski had told him that the ridge was about a mile up the valley. It was almost night and the starlight reflected off the hills lit the valley with fleeting, vivid colours. He ran on heavily, the only sounds he could hear were those of a thresher rattling like a giant metal insect half a mile behind him. Filling his lungs, he pushed on across the last hundred yards.

Kandinski was still lying on the edge of the ridge, watching the space-ship and waiting impatiently for Ward. Below him in the hollow the upper and lower rotor sections swung around more slowly, at about one revolution per second. The space-ship had sunk a further ten feet into the desert floor and he was now on the same level as the observation dome. A single finger of light poked out into the darkness, circling the ridge walls in jerky sweeps.

Then out of the valley behind him he saw someone stumbling along towards the ridge at a broken run. Suddenly a feeling of triumph and exhilaration came over him, and he knew that at last he had his witness.

Ward climbed up the slope to where he could see Kandinski. Twice he lost his grip and slithered downwards helplessly, tearing his hands on the gritty surface. Kandinski was lying flat on his chest his head just above the ridge. Covered by dust, he was barely distinguishable from the slope itself.

'Are you all right?' Ward whispered. He pulled off his bow tie and ripped open his collar. When he had controlled his breathing he crawled up besides Kandinski.

'Where?' he asked.

Kandinski pointed down into the hollow.

Ward raised his head, levering himself up on his elbows. For a few seconds he peered out into the darkness, and then drew his head back.

'You see it?' Kandinski whispered. His voice was short and laboured. When Ward hesitated before replying he suddenly seized Ward's wrist in a vice-like grip. In the faint light reflected by the white dust on the ridge Ward could see plainly his bright inflamed eyes.

'Ward! Can you see it?'

The powerful fingers remained clamped to his wrist as he lay beside Kandinski and gazed down into the darkness.

Below the compartment window one of Ward's fellow passengers was being seen off by a group of friends, and the young women in bright hats and bandanas and the men in slacks and beach sandals made him feel that he was leaving a sea-side resort at the end of a holiday. From the window he could see the observatory domes of Mount Vernon rising out of the trees, and he identified the white brick-work of the Hoyle Library a thousand feet below the summit. Edna Cameron had brought him to the station, but he had asked her not to come onto the platform, and she had said good-bye and driven off. Cameron himself he had seen only once, when he had collected his books from the Institute.

Trying to forget it all, Ward noted thankfully that the train would leave within five minutes. He took his bankbook out of his wallet and counted the last week's withdrawals. He winced at the largest item, 600 dollars which he had transferred to Kandinski's account to pay for the cablegrams.

Deciding to buy something to read, he left the car and walked back to the news-stand. Several of the magazines contained what could only be described as discouraging articles about himself, and he chose two or three newspapers.

Just then someone put a hand on his shoulder. He turned and saw Kandinski.

'Are you leaving?' Kandinsky asked quietly. He had trimmed his beard so that only a pale vestige of the original bloom remained, revealing his high bony cheekbones. His face seemed almost fifteen years younger, thinner and more drawn, but at the same time composed, like that of a man recovering slowly from the attack of some intermittent fever.

'I'm sorry, Charles,' Ward said as they walked back to the car. 'I should have said goodbye to you but I thought I'd better not.'

Kandinski's expression was subdued but puzzled. 'Why?' he asked. 'I don't understand.'

Ward shrugged. 'I'm afraid everything here has more or less come to an end for me, Charles. I'm going back to Princeton until the spring. Freshman physics.' He smiled ruefully at himself. 'Boyle's Law, Young's Modulus, getting right back to fundamentals. Not a bad idea, perhaps.'

'But why are you leaving?' Kandinski pressed.

'Well, Cameron thought it might be tactful of me to leave. After our statement to the Secretary-General was published in *The New York Times* I became very much *persona non grata* at the Hubble. The trustees were on to Professor Renthall again this morning.'

Kandinski smiled and seemed relieved. 'What does the Hubble matter?' he scoffed. 'We have more important work to do. You know, Ward, when Mrs Cameron told me just now that you were leaving I couldn't believe it.'

'I'm sorry, Charles, but it's true.'

'Ward,' Kandinski insisted. 'You can't leave. The Primes will be returning soon. We must prepare for them.'

'I know, Charles, and I wish I could stay.' They reached the car and Ward put his hand out. 'Thanks for coming to see me off.'

Kandinski held his hand tightly. 'Andrew, tell me the truth. Are you afraid of what people will think of you? Is that why you want to leave? Haven't you enough courage and faith in yourself?'

'Perhaps that's it,' Ward conceded, wishing the train would start. He reached for the rail and began to climb into the car but Kandinski held him.

'Ward, you can't drop your responsibilities like this!'

'Please, Charles,' Ward said, feeling his temper rising. He pulled

111

his hand away but Kandinski seized him by the shoulder and almost dragged him off the car.

Ward wrenched himself away. 'Leave me alone!' he snapped fiercely. 'I saw your space-ship, didn't I?'

Kandinski watched him go, a hand picking at his vanished beard, completely perplexed.

Whistles sounded, and the train began to edge forward.

'Good-bye, Charles,' Ward called down. 'Let me know if you see anything else.'

He went into the car and took his seat. Only when the train was twenty miles from Mount Vernon did he look out of the window.

The Killing Ground

As the last smoke from the burning personnel carrier rose through the wet dawn air, Major Pearson could see the silver back of the river three hundred yards from his command post on the hill. Pulverized by the artillery fire, the banks of the channel had collapsed into a network of craters. Water leaked across the meadow, stained by the diesel oil from the fuel tanks of the carrier. Working the binoculars with his thin hands, Pearson studied the trees along the opposite bank. The river was little wider than a stream, and no more than waist-deep, but the fields on both sides were as open as billiard tables. Already the American helicopters had climbed from their bases around the city, clattering in packs over the valley like mindless birds.

An explosion in the driving cabin of the personnel carrier kicked out the doors and windshield. The light flared across the water-soaked meadow, for a moment isolating the faded letters on the memorial stone that formed the rear wall of the command post. Pearson watched the nearest flight of helicopters. They were circling the motor-bridge a mile down-river, too far away to notice the wrecked vehicle and its perimeter of corpses. The ambush, though successful, had not been planned. The carrier had blindly driven up the embankment road as Pearson's unit was preparing to cross the river.

With any luck, Pearson hoped, the crossing would now be called off and they would be ordered to withdraw into the hills. He shivered in his ragged uniform. Corporal Benson had pulled the trousers off a dead Marine machine-gunner the previous morning, and there had been no time to wash out the blood caked across the thighs and waist.

Behind the memorial was the sandbagged entrance of the storage tunnel. Here Sergeant Tulloch and the seventeen-year-old lieutenant sent up overnight from the youth cadre were working on the field radio, rewiring the headphones and battery. Around the emplacement Pearson's thirty men sat over their weapons, ammunition boxes and telephone wire piled around their feet. Exhausted by the ambush, they would have little energy left for a river crossing.

'Sergeant . . . Sergeant Tulloch!' Pearson called out, deliberately coarsening his over-precise schoolmaster's voice. As he half-expected,

Tulloch ignored the shout. A pair of copper terminals clamped in his sharp mouth, he went on splicing the frayed wire. Although Pearson was in command of the guerilla unit, its real initiative came from the Scotsman. A regular in the Gordon Highlanders before the American landings six years earlier, the sergeant had joined the first rebel bands that formed the nucleus of the National Liberation Army. As Tulloch himself openly boasted, he had been drawn to the insurgent army chiefly by the prospect of killing the English. Pearson often wondered how far the sergeant still identified him with the puppet regime in London propped up by the American occupation forces.

As he climbed out of the slit trench gunfire flickered from the central traverse of the motor-bridge. Pearson waited behind the plinth of the memorial. He listened to the roar of heavy howitzers firing from the American enclave five miles to the west. Here nine hundred Marine artillerymen had been holding out for months against two divisions of rebel troops. Supported from the air by helicopter drops, the Americans fought on from their deep bunkers, firing thousands of rounds a day from their seventy guns. The meadows around the enclave formed the landscape of a drowned moon.

The shell whined away through the damp air, the explosions lifting the broken soil. Between the impacts came the rattle of small arms fire as the attack went in across the bridge. Slinging his Sten gun over his narrow shoulders, Pearson ran back to the tunnel.

'What's holding us up, Sergeant? This radio should have been checked at Battalion.'

He reached out to the mud-splattered console, but Tulloch pushed his hand away with the spanner. Ignoring the young lieutenant's self-conscious salute, Tulloch snapped: 'I'll have it ready in time, Major. Or are you wanting to withdraw now?'

Avoiding the lieutenant's eyes, Pearson said: 'We'll follow orders, Sergeant, when and if you repair this set.'

'I'll repair it, Major. Don't worry yourself about that.'

Pearson unfastened the chin-strap of his helmet. During their three months together the sergeant had clearly decided that Pearson had lost heart. Of course Tulloch was right. Pearson looked around the fortified position shielded from the air by the ragged willows, counting the pinched faces of the men huddled beside the field stove. Dressed in ragged uniforms held together with American webbing, living for months in holes in the ground, under-fed and

114

under-armed, what kept them going? Not hatred of the Americans, few of whom, apart from the dead, they had ever seen. Secure within their bases, and protected by an immense technology of warfare, the American expeditionary forces were as remote as some archangelic legion on the day of Armageddon.

If anything, it was fortunate that the Americans were spread so thinly on the ground, or the entire liberation front would long since have been wiped out. Even with twenty million men under arms, the Americans could spare fewer than 200,000 soldiers for the British Isles, a remote backwater in their global war against dozens of national liberation armies. The underground free radio system which Pearson and Tulloch listened to at night as they huddled in their tunnels below the searching helicopters reported continuous fighting from the Pyrenees to the Bavarian Alps, the Caucasus to Karachi. Thirty years after the original conflict in south-east Asia, the globe was now a huge insurrectionary torch, a world Viet Nam.

'Benson!' The corporal limped over, his captured carbine heavy in his thin arms. Pearson waved with a show of temper at the men slumped against the sandbags. 'Corporal, in half an hour we're going into an attack! At least keep them awake!'

With a tired salute, the corporal went off round the emplacement, half-heartedly nudging the men with his boot. Pearson stared through the trees at the river line. To the north, near the ruined castle at Windsor, columns of smoke rose below the helicopters as they plunged and dived, firing their rockets into the ragged forests that had grown among the empty surburban streets. In this immense plain of violence only the meadow below with its leaking river seemed quiet. The water ebbed around the personnel carrier, stirring the legs of the corpses. Without thinking, Pearson started to count his men again. They would have to run across the open ground, ford the river and penetrate the line of trees on the opposite bank. Perhaps the Americans were sitting there with their rapid-fire Gatlings, waiting for them to break cover.

' . . . Major Pearson.' The lieutenant touched his elbow. 'You wanted to see the prisoners.'

'Right. We'll have another go at them.' Pearson followed the boy around the memorial. The presence of this young man – barely older than his pupils at the mountain school in the north of Scotland – gave Pearson some kind of encouragement. Already his age had begun to tell doubly against him. Over the years the losses in manpower had been so great, a million soldiers and a further million civilians dead, that older men were put in the more dangerous roles, saving the young for whatever peace would one day come.

The three Americans were behind the memorial, guarded by a soldier with a Bren gun. Lying on his back was a Negro sergeant who had been shot through the chest. His arms and shoulders were caked with blood, and he breathed unevenly through the thick crust on his mouth and chin. Leaning against him was a young private hunched over the knapsack on his knees. His tired student's eyes stared down at his manacled wrists, as if unable to grasp the fact of his own capture.

The third prisoner was a captain, the only officer in the ambushed patrol, a slimly built man with grey crew-cut hair and a soft but intelligent face. In spite of his uniform and webbing he looked less like a combat soldier than a war correspondent or observer. Telephone wire was lashed around his wrists, forcing him to hold his elbows together. Nevertheless he was watching closely the preparations for the coming attack. Pearson could see him counting the men and weapons, the two machine-guns and ammunition boxes.

As these sharp blue eyes turned to examine Pearson, running over his decrepit uniform and equipment, Pearson felt a surge of resentment at these intelligent and self-confident men who had occupied the world with their huge expeditionary armies. The American was looking at him with that same surprise Pearson had seen on prisoners' faces before, a genuine amazement that these ragged little men could go on fighting for so long. Even the term the Americans used to describe the rebel soldiers 'Charlie', inherited from the first Viet Nam showed their contempt, whether the soldier fighting against them was a Riff tribesman, Catalan farmer or Japanese industrial worker.

However, as the American knew all too well, if the order came through to attack the three of them would be shot down where they sat.

Pearson knelt by the Negro sergeant. With the barrel of his Sten gun he nudged the young soldier clutching his knapsack. 'Can't you do anything for him? Where's your morphine?'

The soldier looked up at Pearson, and then let his head drop, staring at the fuel oil that formed rainbows on his boots. Pearson raised his hand, about to hit him with the back of his fist. Then the

116

sounds of gunfire on the motor-bridge were lost in the overhead whoom of a shell. Coming across the river, the heavy 120 mm soared over the meadow and plunged into the woods below the hill-crest. Pearson crouched behind the memorial, hoping the shell was a stray. Then Sergeant Tulloch signalled that two more had started on their way. The next fell without exploding into the water-meadow. The third landed fifty feet below the memorial, spattering its surface with broken earth.

When it was quiet again Pearson waited as Corporal Benson pulled the knapsack away from the young soldier and emptied its contents. He slit the captain's pockets with his bayonet and jerked off his ID tag.

There was little to be gained from any formal interrogation. American weapons technology had advanced to the point where it made almost no sense at all to the rebel commanders. Artillery fire, battle dispositions and helicopter raids were now computer-directed, patrols and sorties programmed ahead. The American equipment was so sophisticated that even the wrist-watches stripped off dead prisoners were too complicated to read.

Pearson reached down to the clutter of coins and keys beside the private. He opened a leather-bound diary. Inside was a series of illegible entries, and a folded letter from a friend, evidently a draft-dodger, about the anti-war movement at home. Pearson tossed them into the pool of water leaking below the plinth of the memorial. He picked up an oil-stained book, one of a paperback educational series, Charles Olsen's 'Call Me Ishmael.'

As he held the book in his hands, Pearson glanced back to where Sergeant Tulloch stood over the field radio, well aware that the sergeant would disapprove of this unfading strand of literacy in his own character. He wiped the oil off the American eagle. What an army, whose privates were no longer encouraged to carry field-marshals' batons in their knapsacks but books like this.

To the captain he said: 'The US Army must be the most literate since Xenophon's.' Pearson slipped the book into his pocket. The captain was looking down over his shoulder at the river. 'Do you know where we are?' Pearson asked him.

The captain turned himself round, trying to ease the wounds on his wrists. He looked up at Pearson with his sharp eyes. 'I guess so. Runnymede, on the Thames River.'

Surprised, Pearson said ungrudgingly: 'You're better informed than my own men. I used to live about ten miles from here. Near one of the pacified villages.'

'Maybe you'll go back one day.'

'I dare say, Captain. And maybe we'll sign a new Magna Carta into the bargain. How long have you been out here?'

The captain hesitated, sizing up Pearson's interest. 'Just over a month.'

'And you're in combat already? I thought you had a three-month acclimatization period. You must be as badly off as we are.'

'I'm not a combat soldier, Major. I'm an architect, with US Army Graves Commission. Looking after memorials all over the world.'

'That's quite a job. The way things are going, it has almost unlimited prospects.'

'I hate to have to agree with you, Major.' The American's manner had become noticeably more ingratiating, but Pearson was too preoccupied to care. 'Believe me, a lot of us back home feel the war's achieved absolutely nothing.'

'Nothing . . . ?' Pearson repeated. 'It's achieved everything.' An armoured helicopter soared across the hill-crest, its heavy fans beating at the foliage over their heads. For one thing, the war had turned the entire population of Europe into an armed peasantry, the first intelligent agrarian community since the eighteenth century. *That* peasantry had produced the Industrial Revolution. This one, literally burrowing like some advanced species of termite into the sub-soil of the twentieth century, might in time produce something greater. Fortunately, the Americans were protected from any hope of success by their own good intentions, their refusal, whatever the cost in their own casualties, to use nuclear weapons.

Two tanks had moved on to the parapet of the bridge, firing their machine-guns along the roadway. A scout helicopter shot down into the fields across the river was burning fiercely, the flames twisting the metal blades.

'Major!' Corporal Benson ran to the tunnel mouth. Tulloch was crouched over the radio, headphones on, beckoning towards Pearson. 'They're through to Command, sir.'

Ten minutes later, when Pearson passed the memorial on his way to the forward post, the American captain had managed to lift himself on to his knees. Wrists clamped together in front of his chest, he looked as if he were praying at some ruined wayside shrine. The wounded Negro had opened his eyes, shallow breaths breaking through the caked blood on his lips. The young private slept against the plinth of the memorial.

The captain pointed with his wired hands at the men strapping up their packs. Pearson ignored him, and was about to move on. Then something about the American's posture, and their shared community of fatigue and hopelessness, made him stop.

'We're going forward.'

Eyes half-closing, the American stared down at his wrists, as if aware of the effort he had wasted in trying to prevent the abrasions from opening. 'That's bad luck. Not my day.' His face grew stiff and wooden as the blood emptied from his cheeks.

Pearson watched Sergeant Tulloch supervise the stowage of the radio and begin his rounds of the men, waiting with weapons at the ready. 'Why did you come up the river?'

The captain tapped the memorial stone with his wrists. 'We wanted to see about moving this. The Kennedy Memorial.'

'Kennedy . . . ?' Pearson turned and stared down at the broken lettering on the stone. Vaguely he remembered the memorial built by a previous British government at Runnymede to commemorate the assassinated President. In an amiable, if sentimental, gesture an acre of English ground had been given to the American people overlooking Magna Carta island. The President's widow had been present at the unveiling.

The American was feeling the broken lettering. He pulled off his cap and dipped it in the pool of oil-stained water beside the plinth. He began to work away at the memorial, scraping off the mud, as Pearson moved down through the trees to the forward post.

When Pearson returned shortly afterwards the American was still working away at the memorial with his wired hands. Below the surface dirt were the residues of earlier defacements, slogans marked in engine grease or cut with bayonets. There was even one, 'Stop US Atrocities in Viet Nam', almost as old as the monument itself. Pearson remembered that the memorial had been regularly defaced since its unveiling, a favourite target of vandals and agitators.

'Major, we're ready to move off, sir.' Tulloch saluted him smartly, for the first time that day. The American was still scraping at the stone, and had managed to clean at least half of the front surface.

The lead platoon moved down the slope. As the captain dropped his cap and sat down, Pearson signalled to Sergeant Tulloch.

'OK, Charlie – off your backside!' Tulloch had drawn his .45 automatic. The rear platoon was filing past, the men's eyes fixed on the gaps in the trees, none of them paying any attention to the prisoners.

The American stood up, his eyes almost closed. He joined the two prisoners lying behind the memorial. As he began to sit down again Tulloch stepped behind him and shot him through the head. The American fell on to the sleeping private. Tulloch straddled his body with one leg. Like a farmer expertly shearing a sheep he shot the other two men, holding them as they struggled. They lay together at the base of the memorial, their legs streaming with blood.

Above them, the drying stone was turning a pale grey in the weak sunlight.

It was almost white twenty minutes later when they began their advance across the meadow. Fifty yards from the bank a murderous fire had greeted them from the Americans concealed among the trees along the opposite shore. Pearson saw Tulloch shot down into the waterlogged grass. He shouted to Corporal Benson to take cover. As he lay in a shallow crater the white rectangle of the memorial was visible through the trees behind him, clear now as it would not have been that morning. In his last moments he wondered if the cleaning of the memorial had been a signal, which the watching Americans had rightly interpreted, and if the captain had deliberately taken advantage of him.

Mortar shells fell in the damp grass around him. Pearson stood up, beckoning to the young lieutenant to follow him, and ran forward to the wreck of the personnel carrier. Ten steps later he was shot down into the oil-stained water.

One Afternoon at Utah Beach

'Do you realize that we're looking down at Utah Beach?'

As he took off his boots and weather cape, David Ogden pointed through the window at the sea wall. Fifty yards from the villa the flat sand ran along the Normandy coast like an abandoned highway, its right shoulder washed by the sea. Every half-mile a blockhouse of black concrete presented its shell-pocked profile to the calm Channel.

Small waves flicked at the empty beach, as if waiting for something to happen.

'I walked down to the war memorial,' Ogden explained. 'There's a Sherman there – an American tank – some field guns and a commemorative plaque. This is where the US First Army came ashore on D-Day. Angela . . . ?'

Ogden turned from the window, expecting his wife to comment on his discovery. She and Richard Foster, the pilot who had flown them over to Cherbourg for a week at this rented villa, sat at either end of the velvet settee, watching Ogden with a curious absence of expression. Dressed in their immaculate holiday wear, brandy glasses motionless in their hands as they listened politely, they reminded him of two mannequins in a department store tableau.

'Utah Beach . . . ' Angela gazed in a critical way at the deserted sand, as if expecting a military exercise to materialize for her and fill it with landing craft and assault troops. 'I'd forgotten about the war. Dick, do you remember D-Day?'

'I was two.' Foster stood up and strolled to the window, partly blocking Ogden's view. 'My military career began a little later than yours, David.' Glancing down at Ogden, who was now staring at a blockhouse six hundred yards away, he said, 'Utah Beach – well, you wanted some good shooting. Are you sure this isn't Omaha, or one of the others – Juno, Gold, what were they called?'

Without any intended rudeness, Ogden ignored the younger man. His face was still numb from the sea air, and he was intent on his communion with the empty sand and the block-houses. Walking along the beach, he had been surprised by the size of these concrete monsters. He had expected a chain of subterranean pill-boxes hiding within the sea wall, but many of them were massive fortresses three storeys high, larger than the parish churches in the near-by towns. The presence of the blockhouses, like the shells of the steel pontoons embedded in the wet sand, had pulled an unsuspected trigger in his mind. Like all examples of cryptic architecture, in which form no longer revealed function – Mayan palaces, catacombs, Viet Cong sanctuaries, the bauxite mines at Les Baux where Cocteau had filmed *Le Testament d'Orphée* – these World War II blockhouses seemed to transcend time, complex ciphers with a powerful latent identity.

'Omaha is further east along the coast,' he told Foster matter-of-factly. 'Utah Beach was the closest of the landing grounds to Sainte-Mère-Église, where the 82nd Airborne came down. The marshes we shoot across held them up for a while.'

Foster nodded sagely, his eyes running up and down Ogden's slim but hyperactive figure for what seemed the hundredth time that day. Throughout their visit Foster appeared to be sympathetically itemizing a catalogue of his defects, without in any way being insolent. Staring back at him, Ogden reflected in turn that for all the hours Foster had logged as a salesman of executive jets his sallow face remained remarkably pallid as if he were plagued by some deep *malaise*, some unresolvable contradiction. By noon a dark stain seemed to leak from his mouth on to his heavy chin, a shadow that Foster had once described to Angela as a blue tan from spending too much time in bars.

As if separating the two men like a referee, Angela came to the window. 'For someone who's never been in the army or heard a shot fired in anger, David's remarkably well-informed about military matters.'

'Isn't he – for a non-combatant,' Foster agreed. 'And I don't mean that in any critical spirit, David. I spent five years in the army and no one ever told me who won the battle of Waterloo.'

'Weren't you a helicopter pilot?' Ogden asked. 'Actually, I'm not all that interested in military history . . .'

Strictly speaking, this wasn't true, Ogden admitted to himself during lunch, though in fact he had not thought of the D-Day beaches when Angela first suggested the week in Normandy. Under the pretext of a demonstration flight in the twin Comanche, Foster had offered to fly them gratis, though his real reasons were hard to define. The whole trip was surrounded by ambiguities, motives hidden inside each other like puzzle boxes.

This curious threesome – the aircraft salesman, the provincial film critic in his late forties, and the young wife ten years his junior, a moderately successful painter of miniatures – sat in this well-appointed villa beside a long-forgotten battleground as if unsure what had brought them here. Curious, not because of any confrontation that might occur, any crime of passion, but because three people so ill-assorted had formed such a stable relationship. At no time during the six months since their meeting at the San Sebastian festival had there been the slightest hint of tension, though Ogden was sure everyone took for granted that his wife and Richard Foster were well into an affair. However, for various reasons Ogden doubted this. For her own security Angela needed someone around her who had achieved a modest degree of failure.

His young wife . . . Ogden repeated the phrase to himself, realizing as he watched Angela's sharper chin and more prominent jaw muscles, the angular shoulders inside the chiffon blouse, that she was not all that young any more. Soon she would be older than he had been when they first met.

'I'm taking Angela into Sainte-Mère,' Foster told him after lunch. 'Do you want to come along, David? We can try the calvados.'

As usual, Ogden declined. The walk that morning had exhausted him. He stretched out in an armchair and watched the slack sea shrug itself against the beach. He was aware of the complex time-table of apparently arbitrary journeys that Foster and his wife embarked upon each day, but for the moment his attention was held by the blockhouse six hundred yards away. Despite the continuous sunlight the concrete was drenched in spray, gleaming like wet anthracite as if generating its own weather around itself.

An hour after his wife and Foster had gone, Ogden pulled on his boots. He had recovered from the lunch, and the silent villa with its formal furniture felt like the stage-set of a claustrophobic drama. The strong afternoon light had turned the beach into a brilliant mirror, a flare-path beckoning him to some unseen destination.

As he neared the blockhouse Ogden visualized himself defending this battered redoubt against the invading sea. An immense calm presided over the cool beach, as if nothing had happened in the intervening thirty years. The violence here, the scale of the conflict between the German armies and the allied armada, had pre-empted any further confrontation, assuaging his own unease about Foster and his wife.

Fifty yards from the blockhouse he climbed the scrub-covered dune that rose to its seaward flank. The sand was scattered with worn-out shoes, cycle tyres and fragments of wine bottles and vegetable crates. Generations of tramps had used these old forts as staging-posts on their journeys up and down the coast. The remains of small fires lay on the steps of the concrete staircase at the rear of the blockhouse, and pats of dried excrement covered the floor of the munitions store.

Ogden walked across the central gunnery platform of the block-house, a rectilinear vault large enough to house a railway locomotive. From here a heavy-calibre naval gun had lobbed its shells at the invasion fleet. A narrow stairway set into the solid wall climbed to the observation deck, and gave access to the barbette of a small-arms weapons platform below the roof. Ogden climbed the stairway, tripping twice in the darkness. The worn concrete was slick with moisture sweating from its black surface.

As he stood on the roof, lungs pumping in the cold air, the sea already seemed far below, the villa hidden behind its high privet hedges. Looking around, though, he immediately noticed the white Pallas parked behind the sea wall two hundred yards along the beach. The car was the same colour as the Citroën they had hired in Cherbourg, and Ogden took for granted that it was their own vehicle. A tall man in a hunting jacket was steering a woman companion along the broken ground behind the wall. They approached a wooden boathouse at the end of a slipway above the beach, and Ogden could see clearly the patterns of the woman's musquash fur and recognize her gesture as she reached a gloved hand to the man's elbow.

Ogden stepped down into the stairwell. Watching them calmly, his shoulders hidden by the parapet, he knew that he had deliberately encouraged Angela and Richard Foster to come together. His own solitary walks, the private excursions he had made to the D-Day museum at Arromanches, had been part of a confused and half-conscious attempt to bring matters to a head and force a decision on himself.

Yet when he saw them unlocking the door of the boathouse together, briefly embracing in the sunlight as if openly trying to provoke him, Ogden felt a profound sense of loss. He knew too that the months of self-control had been wasted, and that from the beginning he had deluded himself that all was well.

Without thinking, he turned quickly from the parapet. With luck he could pack, call a taxi and have caught the ferry from Cherbourg before they returned to the villa. He started to run down the concrete steps, lost his footing on the damp diagonal sills, and fell backwards down the stairway on to the floor of the barbette ten feet below.

Sitting in the half-light against the wet concrete wall, Ogden massaged his bruised hands. By luck he had been able to protect his head, but he could feel the raw skin of his arms and shoulders. Some sort of viscous oil stained his fawn trousers, and a leather button torn from his jacket lay like a burst chestnut at the foot of the stairway. Immediately to his left was the embrasure of the fire-sill, the quiet beach below. There was no movement from the boathouse, and the white Pallas was still parked behind the sea wall.

At this moment Ogden realized that he was not the only person keeping a close watch on the beach. Six feet away from him, almost hidden by his grey uniform in the shadows behind the parapet, a man lay against the concrete wall. He was resting on one elbow, face turned towards the open sea, and at first Ogden assumed that he was dead. His blond hair had been bleached to an almost arctic pallor. He appeared to be no more than nineteen or twenty years old, his pale skin stretched across the bony points of his face like wet parchment around a skull.

His thin legs, encased in a pair of heavy boots and ragged serge trousers, stuck out in front of him like poles strung with rags. Lying diagonally across them, its long barrel supported by a bipod, was a light machine-gun, stock pressed against the young man's right shoulder. Around him, arranged like the décor of a shabby military display, were an empty mess tin, a spent ammunition belt, the half-rotted remains of a field pack and webbing, and a grease-stained ground sheet.

A few feet from Ogden, lying on the fire-sill within his reach, was a spring-action flare-pistol of a type he had seen only the previous afternoon in the D-Day museum at Arromanches. He recognized it immediately, like the uniform and equipment of this young Wehrmacht soldier whose corpse he had stumbled upon, in some way preserved by the freezing air, or perhaps by the lime leaking from the hastily mixed concrete. Curiously, the machine-gun still appeared to be in working order, a spiked bayonet fitted under the barrel, the butt-stock and receiver greased and polished.

Confused by this macabre discovery, Ogden had already forgotten his wife's infidelity. He was about to pick up the flare-pistol and fire it over the parapet in the direction of the boathouse. But as his bruised hand touched the frozen butt Ogden became aware that the young soldier's eyes were watching him. Of a blanched blue from which almost all pigment had been washed away, they had turned from the beach and were examining Ogden with a tired but steady gaze. Although the soldier's white hands still lay passively at his sides, his right shoulder had moved against the wall, swinging the machine-gun fractionally towards Ogden.

Too frightened to speak, Ogden sat back, taking in every detail of the German's equipment, every ammunition round and piece of webbing, every pore in the cold skin of this young soldier still defending his blockhouse on Utah Beach as he had done in 1944.

After a moment, to Ogden's relief, the machine-gun barrel turned towards the sea. The German had shifted his position slightly, and was once again scanning the beach. His left hand moved to his face, as if he were hoping to transfer a morsel of food to his mouth, and then fell to the floor. A ragged bandage circled his chest, covering a blackened wound partly hidden by his tunic. He took no notice of Ogden as the latter climbed to his feet, both hands pressed to the wall as if frightened that it might collapse on him at any time.

But as Ogden stepped over the machine-gun a white claw moved across the floor, about to seize his ankle.

'*Hören Sie . . .* ' The voice was flat, as if coming off an almost erased recording tape. '*Wieviel Uhr ist es?*' He looked up with a kind of exhausted impatience. '*Verstehen Sie? Quelle heure . . . ? Aujourd'hui? Hier?*' Dismissing Ogden with a wave, he murmured, '*Zu viel Larm . . . zu viel Larm . . .* '

Pulling the stock of the machine-gun into his shoulder, he stared along its barrel at the beach below.

Ogden was about to leave, when a movement on the beach caught his eye. The boathouse door had opened. Richard Foster stepped into the sunlight, and swung his arms lazily in the cool air as he waited until Angela appeared thirty seconds later. Together they walked across the dunes to the parked Pallas, climbed into the car and drove off.

Ogden paused by the staircase, watching the young soldier with the machine gun. He realized that the German had seen neither Foster nor his wife. The boathouse and sea wall were hidden from him by the parapet of the barbette. But if he recovered from his wounds, and moved forward to the edge of the fire-sill . . .

By the time he reached the villa ten minutes later Ogden had already decided on both the tactics and strategy of what he knew would be the last military action of World War II.

'Have you seen the blankets from the children's room?' Angela flicked through the inventory, her sharp eyes watching her husband as he played chess with himself by the sitting-room window. 'I didn't bother to check them when we arrived, but Mme Saunier insists they're missing.'

Ogden looked up from the chessboard. As he shook his head he glanced at the blockhouse. For the three days since his discovery the suspense had become exhausting; at any moment he expected a wounded Wehrmacht soldier to appear on the roof among the wheeling gulls, a pink blanket around his shoulders. At lunch he had changed his place, sitting by himself further down one side of the table so that he could keep the blockhouse under observation.

'Perhaps they were never there,' he said. 'We can replace them.'

'They were here all right. Mme Saunier is scrupulous about this sort of thing. She also said something about one of the decanters. David, are you in a trance?'

Irritably, Angela pushed her blonde hair from her forehead, then gave up and picked up her coat. Richard Foster was waiting by the car in the drive, one of the two shotguns they had hired cradled under his arm. Ogden noticed that he had taken to carrying the weapon everywhere with him, almost as if he detected a change of atmosphere in the villa. In fact, Ogden had gone to strenuous lengths to maintain the good humour of the first days of their holiday.

He waited patiently for them to leave. Half an hour later Mme Saunier set off in her Simca. When the sounds of the car had faded Ogden stood up and moved swiftly across the villa to the conservatory at the rear of the dining-room. He removed the pots of bright winter plants standing on the wooden dais, eased back the platform from the wall and pulled out the cheap suitcase he had bought in Sainte-Mère that morning while Angela and Foster were lounging over the breakfast table. Taking the blankets from the empty bedroom had been a mistake, but at the time he had been concerned only to keep the young soldier alive.

Inside the suitcase were adhesive tape, sterile lint and antiseptic cream, one bottle of Vichy water and a second of schnapps, a primus stove, six cans of assorted soup, and a pull-through he had purchased from the town's gunsmith. However carefully the German had oiled the machine-gun, its barrel would need a thorough reaming-out.

After checking the contents, Ogden replaced the dais and let himself through the conservatory doors. Protected by the high privets, the garden was warm, and the air coming off the beach had an almost carnival sparkle. As usual, though, by the time he reached the blockhouse the temperature had dropped by almost ten degrees, as if this black concrete redoubt existed within a climatic zone of its own.

Ogden paused by the staircase, listening for the sounds of any intruders. On the first afternoon, when he had snatched the children's blankets, flung together an emergency meal of bread, milk and salami, and raced back along the beach to the blockhouse, the German had relapsed into one of the intermittent comas into which he would sink without warning. Although still staring at the tide-line, right hand clasped around the trigger butt of the machine-gun, his face was so cold and pallid that Ogden at first thought he had died. But he revived at the sound of the milk pouring into his mess tin, sat up and allowed Ogden to drape the blankets around his shoulders. Unable to stay more than an hour for fear of alerting his wife, Ogden had spent the evening in a state of hyper-excitability, for some reason terrified that the local police and members of a German military mission might arrive at any moment.

By the next morning, after Ogden had taken the car to Sainte-Mère on the pretext of visiting the war cemeteries there, the German had visibly improved. Although barely aware of Ogden, he leaned more comfortably against the damp wall. He held the mess tin against his bandaged chest, picking at the remains of the sausage. His face had more colour, and the skin was less tightly stretched against the jaw and cheekbones.

The German was often irritated by Ogden's fumbling, and there was something strangely vulnerable about his extreme youth. Ogden visited him twice each day, bringing water, food and cigarettes, whatever he could smuggle out of the villa under the suspicious eyes of Mme Saunier. He would have liked to light a fire for the soldier, but the primus stove he had brought with him on this fourth morning would generate a little warmth. However, the German had survived in this cold – the thought of living through all those winters made Ogden shudder – and at least the summer was coming.

When he climbed the stairway to the barbette the German was sitting up, blankets around his shoulders, quietly cleaning the machine-gun. He nodded to Ogden, who sat panting on the cold floor, and continued to strip the breech, apparently uninterested in the primus stove. When Ogden handed over the pull-through the German glanced at him with a flicker of appreciation. He ate only when he had reassembled the weapon.

Ogden watched him approvingly, relieved to see the young soldier's total dedication to his defence of this lonely strongpoint. It was this kind of courage that Ogden most admired. Earlier he had feared that once the German had recovered his strength he might decide to leave, or fall back to a more defensible position. Clearly he had missed the actual landings on Utah Beach and had no idea that he alone was keeping the war going. Ogden had no intention of telling him the truth, and the German's resolve never wavered.

Despite his overall improvement, the German's legs still seemed useless, and he had not moved forward sufficiently to see the boat-house two hundred yards away. Each afternoon Angela and Richard Foster climbed the dunes to this wooden shack on its miniature wheels, and disappeared into it for an hour. At times, as he waited for them to emerge, Ogden was tempted to wrest the machine-gun from the wounded German and empty its ammunition belt through the flaking weather-board. But the young soldier's aim was probably sharper and more steady. The flare-pistol lay on the fire-sill, the shell in its barrel. When the German had cleaned it they would be ready.

Two days later, soon after one o'clock in the afternoon, began the last military engagement to take place on Utah Beach.

At eleven o'clock that morning, as Angela sat at the breakfast table reading the local French newspaper, Richard Foster returned from the telephone in the hall.

'We'll have to leave this afternoon. The weather's closing in.'

'What?' Ogden left his chess table and joined them in the dining-room. He pointed to the brilliant sunlight falling on the wet satin of the beach. 'It doesn't look like it.'

'I've just talked to the met. people at Cherbourg Airport. There's a front coming in from the Scillies. The barometer's going up like a lift.'

Ogden clasped his hands, trying to control them. 'Well, let's put it off for a day. The plane's fully instrumented.'

'Not a chance. By this time tomorrow the Channel will be packed with cumulo-nimbus. It'll be like trying to fly through a maze of active volcanoes.'

'Dick knows what he's doing,' Angela confirmed. 'I'll read the inventory with Mme Saunier after lunch. She can take the keys to the agents when we've gone.' To Ogden, who was still staring uncertainly at Richard Foster, she said, 'A day won't matter, David. You've done nothing all week but play about on the beach by yourself.'

For the next half an hour Ogden tried to find some excuse for them to stay, pacing up and down the sitting room as suitcases were dragged around upstairs. He tried to shut the two women's voices out of his mind, realizing that his entire scheme was about to fall to pieces. Already he had made his morning visit to the blockhouse, taking coffee, soup and cigarettes. The young German had almost recovered, and had moved the machine-gun closer to the parapet. Now Ogden would have to leave him there. Within days he would realize that the war was over and hand himself in to the French authorities.

Behind him the front door closed. Ogden heard Foster's voice in the drive, Angela calling to him about something. He watched them from the window, in a flat way admiring their nerve. They were setting off for their last walk together, Foster holding Angela's elbow in one hand, the shot-gun in the other.

Still surprised by the blatant way in which they were advertising their affair – during the past two days they had done everything but get into Angela's bed together – Ogden pressed his hands against the window. A faint chance still remained. He remembered the almost provocative way in which Angela had watched him across the dining-table the previous evening, confident that he would do absolutely nothing . . .

Fifteen minutes later Ogden had left the house and an exasperated

Mme Saunier, and was running head down, shot-gun in hand, through the pools of water which the stiffening sea had swilled across Utah Beach.

'Langsamer! Zu schnell. Langsam . . . '

Trying to calm Ogden, the young German raised a white hand and gestured him away from the parapet. He reached forward and shifted the bipod, swinging the machine-gun to take in the section of beach containing the boathouse, at which Ogden had been gesticulating since his arrival.

Ogden crouched against the wall, only too ready to let the German take command. The young soldier's recovery in the space of a few days had been remarkable. Though his hands and face retained their albino-like whiteness, he seemed almost to have put on weight. He moved easily around the fire-sill, in complete control of his heavy weapon. The bolt was cocked back, trigger set for automatic fire. A kind of wan smile, an ironic grimace, hung about his cold mouth, as if he too knew that his long wait was about to come to an end.

Ogden nodded encouragingly, holding his shotgun in as military a grip as he could muster. Its fire-power was nothing by comparison with the German's machine-gun, but it was all he could offer. In some obscure way he felt obligated to this young soldier, and guilty at implicating him in what would in a sense be the last war crime committed during World War II.

'They're – Look!' Ogden ducked behind the parapet, gesturing frantically. The boathouse door had opened, a cracked glass pane throwing a blade of sunlight at them. Ogden lifted himself on to his knees, the flare-pistol in both hands. The German had come to life, moving with professional command, all trace of his injuries forgotten. He adjusted his rear sight, his bandaged shoulder traversing the heavy weapon. Angela and Richard Foster stepped through the door of the boathouse. They paused in the sunlight, Foster casually inspecting the near-by dunes. The shotgun rested on his shoulder, trigger guard clasped around two fingers.

Unnerved for a moment by this aggressive stance, Ogden raised the flare-pistol, cocked the trigger and fired the fat shell into the air over Foster's head. The pilot looked up at its weak parabola, then ran forward, shouting to Angela as the shell lost height and fell like a dead bird into the calm sea.

'A dud . . . !' Angry with himself, Ogden stood up in the embrasure, his head and chest exposed. Raising the shotgun, he fired the left barrel at Foster, who was darting through the dunes little more than a hundred yards from the blockhouse. Beside Ogden the young German was taking aim. The long barrel of the machine-gun followed the running figure. At last he opened fire, the violent noise jarring the parapet. Ogden was standing in the embrasure, happily listening to the roar of the machine-gun, when Richard Foster stood up in the long grass ten yards from the blockhouse and shot him through the chest.

'Is he . . . ?'

Angela waited in the dim light by the stairway, the collar of her fur coat pressed against her cheeks. Avoiding the body on the floor of the barbette, she watched Foster rest his shotgun against the wall and kneel on the floor.

'Stand back as far as you can.' Foster waved her back. He examined the body, then touched the flare-pistol with a blood-stained shoe. He was still shaking, both from fear and from the exhaustion of the past week. By contrast, Angela was completely calm. He noticed that with characteristic thoroughness she had insisted on climbing the stairway.

'It's a damn lucky thing he fired that first, I might not have had time otherwise . . . But where the hell did he find it? And all this other equipment?'

'Let's leave and call the police.' Angela waited, but Foster was still searching the floor. 'Dick! An hour from now I may not sound very convincing.'

'Look at this gear – World War II webbing, machine-gun ammunition, primus stove, German phrase-book and all these cans of soup . . . '

'He was camping here. I told you it would take a lot to provoke him.'

'Angela!' Foster stepped back and beckoned her towards him. 'Look at him . . . For God's sake, he's wearing a German uniform. Boots, tunic, the whole thing.'

'Dick!'

As they made their way from the blockhouse, the alarmed figure of Mme Saunier was hurrying along the beach towards them. Foster held Angela's arm.

'No. Are you all right?'

'Of course.' With a grimace, Angela picked her way down the grimy concrete steps. 'You know, he must have thought we were coming ashore. He was always talking about Utah Beach.'

The 60 Minute Zoom

2.15 P.M.
Lloret de Mar, Apartamentos California

I am looking into a silent world. Through the viewfinder of this cine-camera, set at its maximum field, I can see the Hotel Coral Playa three hundred yards along the beach, covered by a desert light so glazed that it would embalm Pharoah. It's hard to believe that the sea is only a few feet to the right of frame – with this dense powdery light we could be at Karnak, in that tourist hotel by the necropolis where Helen befriended her Stuttgart dentist and first set in train this epic of the amateur camera. The ultimate home movie, perhaps, but so far everything has gone well, thanks to $2500's worth of Nikon Zoomatic and an obliging Barcelona camera specialist. Renting this apartment was the only difficult moment – delivering a second key to my door, did the suspicious Swedish manager catch a glimpse of the complex tripods and clamps I was assembling by the bedroom window? Like the barbette of some sinister assassination weapon, which it is in a way. But this second-rate apartment building provides the only suitable vantage point. The fifteen-storey facade of the Coral Playa must exactly fill the opening sequence – in an hour the automatic zoom will carry me along the carretera, past the hundreds of parked cars and beached speedboats, to within three feet of my target within the bedroom of our tenth-floor hotel suite. A miracle of Japanese lens-cutting. Thinking of the electrifying image, worthy of Bergman or Polanski, that will be the climax of this film almost derails my mind. I listen to the faint susurrus of the zoom motor, the sound of well-bred Osaka matrons at a flower-arrangement course. Despite everything, the degrading but exciting months of anger and suspicion, I feel the first hint of an erection.

2.19 P.M.

Already I am closer to the Coral Playa, the equivalent of perhaps 200 yards away. For the first time I can pick out our own suite, Helen's black water-skis arranged like runes on the balcony. Now and then something flicks through the afternoon light, a bottle-top or cigarette packet flung from one of the unseen apartment blocks on the left. Lying here on a raised couch in the darkened bedroom it is hard to believe that the Coral Playa exists at all except as a figment of this view-finder. But the rectilinear façade of the hotel is sharper. The fifteen floors are each taking on a separate identity. There are differences of tone, subtle declensions of balcony geometry that hint at the personalities of the people behind them. The varying angles of the shutters, the beach umbrellas and bikinis hanging on improvised lines, constitute an elaborate personal notation, a complex of ciphers that would send a semiologist into trance. Almost no sky surrounds the hotel, and half the lurid electrographic sign on the roof has been cut away. The image of the hotel's façade, its 150 balconies, is an increasingly abstract entity. As yet there is no sign of movement – Helen will still be on the bed where I left her, a towel around her head, reading her shower-damp copy of American *Vogue* as I set off ostensibly for Barcelona. The guests are still finishing their gaspacho and paella in the hotel restaurant. In the main ground-floor entrance I can identify several of my neighbours sitting in the armchairs and talking to the lobby clerks. They resemble bored marionettes, unable to sustain their roles in this drama in which I have cast them. My main concern is with the two balconies of our suite and the cluster of adjacent rooms. Already the dark interiors are beginning to lighten, I can just distinguish the internal doors that lead to bathrooms and corridors . . .

Wait . . . While my attention is fixed on my own bedroom, impatient for Helen to make her first appearance as the star of this film, I almost fail to notice that a man in a red bath-robe is standing on a balcony five floors above. An American journalist named Anderson, he is looking down at the entrance drive, where a black Mustang has pulled into one of the diagonal parking spaces. The over-heated carapace is about to flow like tar, and for a moment I am too distracted to notice the young man hefting flippers and snorkel from the rear seat. Rademaekers! Panicking, I realize that the young Danish heart surgeon has returned half an hour earlier than I estimated. My zoom may close in on a shot bolt!

2.24 P.M.

I have calmed myself, straightened the damaged blind and re-aligned the tripod. In the last few minutes the scene before me has been totally transformed. Rademaekers has gone straight to the American's room, where he wanders about gesticulating with the flippers. Drink in hand, he seems unlikely to be visiting Helen in the next hour. The Nikon purrs smoothly, carrying me ever nearer the Coral Playa. Little more than an apparent hundred yards from me, the hotel has become a hive of activity as the guests return from the dining-room and prepare for siesta. Already I recognize dozens of my neighbours in their bedrooms, the men taking off their shoes, the women testing the beach-towels on the balconies and examining their teeth in the dressing-table mirrors. These commonplace but almost meaningless activities have an extraordinary fascination, for years I have watched them in a hundred hotels. For once I am glad that Helen has failed to make her entrance. With her entrenched rationality, her over-calculated approach to life in general and the needs of her sexuality in particular, she has always failed to understand the real significance of my obsession with the private behaviour of my neighbours. She cannot grasp that this aimless minor traffic around their bodies, the applications of sun-oil, the dabbing of scent into this or that fossa, represent a continuing authentication of their physical selves, a non-vocal gossip about their armpits and pudenda that no kinaesthetic language, beyond those provided by the instructions on a deodorant or lady-shaver, has yet been found to express. Fifty units of intense private activity, they edge closer to me. On the second floor the young wife of a Marseilles lawyer undresses to reveal a breastless brown body like a catamite's, sits in bed with the sheet over her knees forming a white pyramid, a geometry of remarkable chasteness from which I move my eyes only when I notice that, at last, the central balcony of the film has been mounted by my wife.

2.28 P.M.

A shame that there is no sound-track. Rather than the Polanski or Fellini of the home movie I shall have to become its D.W. Griffith. With his architectural obsessions he would have appreciated the special merits of this film. I am now looking at the façade of the Coral Playa from a distance of fifty yards. Half a dozen floors are visible, a cluster of balconies at whose centre stands my wife. Wayward and erotic, faithless spouse but excellent travelling companion, she is gazing uncannily, straight towards my camera. The powdery light has cleared, and every detail of the hotel is exposed with the vividness of an hallucination – the rust stains leaking from the balcony rails, the drying swim-suits and discarded paperbacks on the balcony tables, the unfamiliar brands of towel picked up in some provincial Mono-Prix. Oblivious of this plethora of detail swarming around her, Helen is brushing her hair with a reflex hand, revealing the strong muscles of her neck and making the greatest play with her profile for the benefit of the audience watching her from the balconies above and below. For all this attention, she is dressed discreetly in my white towelling robe, no doubt a signal to someone in my absence. Moving my eyes from her, I notice that on the surrounding balconies stands the full complement of her admirers, that troupe of beach-partners one of whom will play the supporting role in this film. Penelope with her suitors, and I with my Nikon-bow. Even the ever-faithful Argus is there in the bedroom behind her, the dented but still inflated rubber sea-lion which Helen bought me, with cruel irony, two years ago at Venice Lido, and which I, refusing to be outdone, have cared for devotedly ever since, much to her exasperation . . .

2.32 P.M.

Helen has loosened my beach-robe, exposing the entire upper hemisphere of her right breast. There is a quickening of heads and eyes. I feel a familiar surge of excitement as I make a last inventory of my rivals. Rademaekers, the pedantic Danish surgeon who took her snorkelling yesterday, has returned to his room three floors diagonally above ours. Even as he hunts for a clean shirt in his wardrobe he is still holding one of the flippers, like a sea-born land creature clinging obsessively to an obsolete organ. I eliminate him, and move to his neighbour, a thirty-year-old Brighton antique dealer, whose speedboat, during our first week, sat reversing in the shallows ten yards from the beach where Helen and I lay under our umbrellas. Engaging but unscrupulous, he too is taking in his opposition – principally Fradier, the Paris comic-strip publisher two floors above, leaning on his balcony rail beside his attractive wife while openly admiring Helen. But Fradier is moving out of frame, and by the logic of this film can be dropped from the cast-list. As the camera moves nearer I approach the main stage of this vertical drama – a tier of fifteen balconies distributed among five floors, Helen at the centre. Two floors below her, bare-chested in the fierce sunlight, is a minor Italian film actor who arrived only yesterday, bringing with him an anthology of dubious sexual techniques which he had

137

already displayed for Helen in the hotel bar after dinner. His profession would make him my chief suspect, but he too is about to move out of frame, exiting from this reductive fable . . .

Helen is scrutinizing her eyes in a lacquered hand-mirror. She plucks a stray hair from her brow-line with the ruthlessness she always applies to her own body. Even thirty feet away, hovering in the air like an invisible angel, I find this violence unnerving. I realize that I have only been fully at ease with my wife while watching her through the viewfinder of a camera – even within the private space of our various hotel rooms I prefer her seen through a lens, emblematic of my own needs and fantasies rather than existing in her own right. At one time this rightly outraged her, but recently she has begun to play along with my obsession. For hours I watch her, picking her nose and arguing with me about something as I lie on the bed with a camera to my eye, fascinated by the shifting geometries of her thighs and shoulders, the diagrams of her face.

Helen has left the balcony. She tosses the mirror on to the bed, gazes with a pensive frown at the fading but still cheerful expression on the face of the sea-lion, and walks straight through the suite to the front door. Almost before I stifle a shout she has disappeared into the corridor. For the moment I am paralyzed. Under my beach robe she is naked.

2.36 P.M.

Where is she? The camera is closing with the Coral Playa at an unsettling speed. I wonder if the Nikon engineers have at last over-reached themselves. I seem to be no more than ten feet from the facade of the hotel, I can almost reach out and touch the balconies. Only three of the suites are now in frame, our own sandwiched between the Lawrences above us, an affable English couple from Manchester, and a forty-year-old Irish pharmacologist below with whom we have made no contact. These three have involuntarily gate-crashed their way into my film. Meanwhile Helen could be anywhere in the hotel, with Rademaekers or the antique dealer, even with the comic-strip publisher if Mme Fradier has left for the beach. Fumbling with the tripod, I am about to realign the camera when Helen reappears, standing in the centre of the Lawrences' sitting room. Barefoot, hands in the pockets of my white beach-robe, she is talking to Lawrence, a handsome, sandy-haired accountant wearing nothing more than a string swim-slip over his ample crutch. But where is his wife? Is she in the hotel pool, or hidden from me by the lowered bedroom shutter, joining in the conversation through the open door? Confused by this unlikely tryst, I am ready to stop the camera when Lawrence and Helen embrace. I catch my breath, but their kiss is merely a light peck. With a wave, Helen takes a magazine from him and steps into the corridor. Thirty seconds later, as Lawrence wanders around the sitting room patting his groin, Helen re-enters our suite. After a pause, she leaves the door ajar. Her actions are calm and unrushed, but totally conspiratorial. With aching relief, my loins are at full cock long before the heavily built figure of the Irish pharmacologist steps deferentially into the sitting-room and locks the door behind him.

2.42 P.M.

Reverie of pain, lust and, above all, child-like hate, in which the slights and antagonisms of a lifetime are subsumed in this unresolvable confrontation between fear and desire, the need and refusal to face the basilisk stare of Helen's sexuality . . . all these modulated by the logic of the zoom, by the geometries of balconies and the laminated gleam of a fashion magazine on a white sheet, the terrifying reductive authority of the encroaching lens. By now the entire frame of the viewfinder is filled by our hotel suite, I seem to be no more than three feet from the nearer of the two balconies, watching Helen and her lover like a theatre-goer in a front stall. So close am I that I fully expect them to incorporate me in their dialogue. Still wearing my beach-robe, Helen strolls around the sitting-room, talking away matter-of-factly as if demonstrating a new domestic appliance to a customer. The pharmacologist sits on the white plastic settee, listening to her in an agreeable way. There is an unforced casualness, a degree of indifference so marked that it is hard to believe they are about to copulate on my bed. Leached away by the camera lens, the dimension of depth is missing from the room, and the two figures have an increasingly abstract relationship to each other, and to the rectilinear forms of the settee, walls and ceiling. In this context almost anything is possible, their movements are a series of postural equations that must have some significance other than their apparent one. As the man lounges back Helen slips off my robe and stands naked in front of him, pointing to the burn marks left by her shoulder straps.

139

2.46 P.M.

For the first time the camera lens has crossed the balcony and entered the domain of our hotel suite. I am no more than a few steps from the Irishman, who is undressing beside the bed, revealing a muscular physique of a kind that has never previously appealed to Helen. She sits naked on the bidet in the bathroom, clearly visible through the open door, picking at a toe-nail and staring with a preoccupied expression at the rubber floor-mat. The white porcelain of the bidet, the chromium fitments and the ultramarine tiles of the bathroom together make a curiously formalized composition, as if Vermeer himself had been resurrected and turned loose to recreate his unhurried domestic interiors in the Delft Hilton. Already I feel my anger begin to fade. Annoyingly, my erection also slackens. The transit of this camera across the last forty minutes, which should have brought me to a positive Golgotha of last humiliation, has in fact achieved a gradual abstraction of emotion, an assuagement of all anger and regret. In a way, I feel a kind of affection for Helen.

2.52 P.M.

They lie together on the bed, taking part in a sexual act so relaxed that this camera should film them in slow motion. I am now so close that I might be sitting in the armchair beside the bed. Enlarged by the lens, the movements of their bodies resemble the matings of clouds. Steadily they inflate before me, the vents of their mouths silently working like those of sleeping fish, a planet of anatomical abstractions on which I will soon land. When they come, our orgasms seem to take place in the air above the bed, like the aerial copulation of exotic and gentle birds. Little more than three feet from the camera, the blurred smile of the sea-lion presides over this interlude of nuptial bliss.

2.56 P.M.

Helen is alone now. Her face is out of frame, and through the viewfinder I see only a segment of the pillow, an area of crumpled sheet and the upper section of her chest and shoulders. An almost undifferentiated whiteness fills the lens, marred by the blue hollow of her armpit and the damp sulcus of her right breast, in which a few of the pharmacologist's hairs have been caught. Edging closer, I watch the easy rise and fall of her rib-cage . . .

Helen has sat up. Breaking this extended calm, she has turned on one elbow. The sharp movement almost jars the camera, and I realize that far from being asleep she has been lying there fully awake, thinking to herself about something. Her face fills the viewfinder, in the only true close-up of this film. She is looking me straight in the eye, violating our never-spoken agreement in a blatant way. In a blur of light I see her hand pull the sea-lion towards her, then stab with her nails at its worn eyes. Instantly it buckles as the air spurts from the dented plastic.

At this moment I am certain that she has known about this film all along, as she must have known about the others I have made, first with the still Hasselblad as she and the young waiter flirted around the Pontresina ski-lift, later following the Bayreuth Kappellmeister with a cheap cine-camera mounted in the back of the car, productions that have increased in both range and ambition as they led to this present most elaborate exercise of all. But even now, I dream of the ultimate voyeurist film, employing bizarre lenses that reach to some isolated balcony over extraordinary distances, across the Bay of Naples to Capri, or from Dover to a beach hotel in Calais, magnifying the moment of orgasm to a degree of absolute enlargement where the elements of her infidelity become totally abstracted from themselves, areas of undifferentiated light that assuage all anger.

3.05 P.M.

Within a few seconds the camera will reach the limits of its zoom. Helen sleeps on her side with her face away from me. Never faltering, the camera creeps onwards, excluding more and more details from the edges of its frame, the stray hairs of her lover, the damp sweat-prints of her shoulder blades on the sheet. Yet I am aware that there has been a sudden intrusion into the white spaces of the bedroom. What are unmistakably parts of a man's shoes and trousers have appeared soundlessly beside the bed, pausing by the sagging beach-toy. Helen sleeps on, her malice forgotten, unaware of the flash of chromium light that irradiates the screen. Fascinated, with no sense of alarm, I watch the movements of this mysterious intruder, the articulated volumes of almost unrelated forms. Only a white field is now visible, detached from all needs and concessions, a primed canvas waiting for its first brush stroke. Applauding, I see the screen fill with sudden red.

The man kneels beside the bed, watching the elaborate patterns formed by the quiet blood as it runs across the sheet, hunting a hundred gradients. As he turns, exposing his face to the camera, I recognize myself. The sea-lion, my faithful Argus, expires at my feet. As always when I see this film and listen to its commentary, the infinite dream of the sixty-minute zoom, I remember the long journey across the dust and noise of Lloret, past the clamour of the sea to the serene world within this hotel bedroom, to my faithful wife rediscovered in the marriage of red and white.

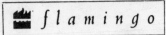

Flamingo is a quality imprint publishing both fiction and non-fiction. Below are some recent titles.

Fiction
- [ ] News From a Foreign Country Came *Alberto Manguel* £4.99
- [ ] The Kitchen God's Wife *Amy Tan* £4.99
- [ ] Moon Over Minneapolis *Fay Weldon* £5.99
- [ ] Isaac and His Devils *Fernanda Eberstadt* £5.99
- [ ] The Crown of Columbus *Michael Dorris & Louise Erdrich* £5.99
- [ ] The Cat Sanctuary *Patrick Gale* £5.99
- [ ] Dirty Weekend *Helen Zahavi* £4.50
- [ ] Mary Swann *Carol Shields* £4.99
- [ ] Cowboys and Indians *Joseph O'Connor* £5.99
- [ ] The Waiting Years *Fumiko Enchi* £5.99

Non-fiction
- [ ] The Proving Grounds *Benedict Allen* £5.99
- [ ] The Quantum Self *Danah Zohar* £4.99
- [ ] Ford Madox Ford *Alan Judd* £6.99
- [ ] C. S. Lewis *A. N. Wilson* £5.99
- [ ] Into the Badlands *John Williams* £5.99
- [ ] Dame Edna Everage *John Lahr* £5.99
- [ ] Handel and His World *H. C. Robbins Landon* £5.99
- [ ] Taking It Like a Woman *Ann Oakley* £5.99

You can buy Flamingo paperbacks at your local bookshop or newsagent. Or you can order them from Fontana Paperbacks, Cash Sales Department, Box 29, Douglas, Isle of Man. Please send a cheque, postal or money order (not currency) worth the purchase price plus 24p per book (maximum postage required is £3.00 for orders within the UK).

NAME (Block letters)_____

ADDRESS_____

_____

_____